CATFISH HONEYTRAP

Table of Contents

Catfish Honeytrap 1
Chapter 1 5
Chapter 2 14
Chapter 3 24
Chapter 4 38
Chapter 5 64
Chapter 6 85
Chapter 7 93
Chapter 8 112
Chapter 9 127
Chapter 10 142
Chapter 11 162
Chapter 12 171
Chapter 13 180

Catfish Honeytrap

Book One of the Confessional Thriller Series

Camren Walker

Estella Publishing

CAMREN WALKER

All characters appearing in this work are fictitious. Any resemblance to real persons, living or dead, is purely coincidental.

Copyright © Camren Walker 2025
All Rights Reserved
ISBN 978-1-0685888-7-7

CATFISH HONEYTRAP

London 2011

When social media wasn't toxic ...

CAMREN WALKER

Chapter 1

'Sorry do you mind if I just lay on the carpet one sec to stretch out my arms and legs? I'm dyspraxic so it's the only way I can sense how much space there is'.

The estate agents's eyes glaze over with a *sure* as she leaves me to it. I've just bought myself an extra few seconds alone in each room. Bitchface has left a loose-corked bottle of her Barrolo wine perching on the coffee table. There are two drawers underneath. I take out the Canadian white dildo and leave it inside the left one. I never had a dildo with Jon so the recriminations should be stronger. I am tempted to knock the Barrolo accidentally on purpose over her luxury white rug. I want to see a red stain and wait to spot it washed or replaced on her next Facebook post. It could be collateral evidence of some hook-up's lovemaking. But I'm not a complete maniac.

She dresses the normal way for someone about to turn thirty. I take some cues from her footwear and memorise the brand-names on the labels on her outfits dangling in her wardrobe. There is just enough room for an IKEA double steel bed. Behind it lie some slatted louvre doors with shallow space for a shoe-rack probably. A make-up bag lies next to the side – her side? – of the double bed. As the estate agent is still a few seconds behind me, I flop silently onto the bed to imprint the sheets with a foreign body. After getting up I yank the chocolates out of my handbag and slip them under her pillow. Then I take out the small bottle of lube. I emptied half of it before coming to the appointment, to make it seem like an active lube bottle. I slip into to make-up bag just as the estate agent appears at the door behind me. As I'm still bending over I take a peek inside the make-up bag, without really noticing the cosmetics she uses.

'Oh, she's got nice cosmetics, too. Sorry just being nosey.'

The agent gives me a dead-eyed smile. I brush past her to get another headstart. The bathroom viewing confirms my worst suspicion.

The shaving gel Jon always uses is there, along with his bathrobe. I place a foreign deodorant behind Jon's and pull the M&S boxer shorts out of my handbag. I was wearing them all night so they should have an incriminating used feel. I drop them behind her washbasket. I notice her period knickers in there. I don't get the chance to take any pics for any future blackmail. The estate agent's small and beady eyes seem to say *off you fuck, timewaster*. I mumble my excuses and leave. Immediately my mind loses track of all the clothes and accessories I was going to imitate, as if they could make me travel back four months in time and erect a parallel dimension in which my ex and bitchface never met.

    I go straight home and sit bolt upright at my desk for what seems like hours. My palm is clinging moistly to the mouse, his mouse. My eyes are glaring at the computer. His computer. Jon's downpayment for moving in together has turned into his parting gift. Spending two hours cyberstalking the woman who stole my boyfriend is not filling the void in my soul. That emptiness is the size of half a human life. Luckily I have a best friend who can can read my mind. When I leave Fiona a voicemail asking if I'm actually mental, about whether it's normal to make a flat-viewing appointment using a fake name, she is ringing my Nokia only a minute later. When she lets herself in my eyes glisten open. I'm no longer the come-over friend hovering over her wine fridge or getting lost in her wide right-angled sofa. She's at my bedsit and I see her again as if for the first time. I am enamoured of the hole in her jeans, clothes five years too young for someone like me in her late twenties. Her inevitable hug envelops me even before her calming words. The stench comes off her from the outside nicotine mixed with alcohol from last night.

    'It's normal to feel pain, hun'.

    She draws out 'pain' with an uplifted tone, as if she's suggesting Spain for a city break. Then she strokes my arm a little, as if spreading avocado on her flatbread.

CATFISH HONEYTRAP

We go to our local Pizza Hut. Pizza Express thinks it's a class apart just because it doesn't put pictures on its menus. But Pizza Hut has buffet time. I go for the extra deep Meat Feast. I go for a second plate and Fiona comes for a further slice in solidarity. We do this once a month and it's one of her ways of slumming it. But I take my buffets seriously and I go for a third plate, not caring how sick I'm going to feel later.

'I still love him', I confess. 'He only fucking dumped me three days ago and this bitchface woman's put her flat on the market. All his stuff's there'.

Fiona's chewing noisily as usual. But her green eyes are open in empathy.

'She took Jon from me, so I have a moral right to, yeah? I wasn't breaking in, just pretending to be a buyer'

'Yep. Not your fault, hun', she says, looking closer at her phone. 'I think I found her on Facebook. This her?.'

Fiona turns her wifi-enabled smartphone to face me. It shows this bitchface woman pouting her lips and wearing a figure-hugging dress.

'Fuck. Yes, that's her.' My gaze lingers, as if finding faults in her might re-set my life several weeks and make Jon see sense.

'She's vain and bling, hun. All tits and Chanel bags. What is she, Korean, Chinese?'.

'That was enough for Jon', I sigh. I place the half-eaten pizza triangle on my plate. 'Oh Chinese, from Hong Kong'.

'Look. I'll add her hun. She's using some of the brands I've been working with. If it's me adding her she won't suspect anything'.

'OK, but what about Jon? Won't she see your Facebook friends with him?'

'No problem. I'm adding her, then unfriending Jon. She'll just think I'm a stranger into her Chanel bags'.

I keep staring at my friend. She has come up with a way of checking up on her in the time it took me to digest a mouthful of pizza. Why did I waste £100 planting elaborate evidence when I could have set up a social media psy-op instead?

'Set up a fake account yourself. She's bound to block you hun unless she thinks you're someone else. It's not stalking. Faye. You're just being nosey.'

I'm taken aback by Fiona's debonnaire instruction. But she is in social media marketing in a trans-Atlantic engagement, so I'm going along with it. After two hours of chat, my ploy for revenge is fleshed out. *Start being vague and demure*, Fiona assures me. I mimic saying *vague and demure* in her voice and it gives her a laugh, a real laugh that takes over her face in a smile. Vague and demure she says would give the impression that I've got other things to do, maybe even a relationship of my own. So like all dumped women, I decide to become a Facebook stalker.

When I get home I pull my curtains and leave my TV lingering on *Grand Designs*. A missed call from Fiona and then a text summons my arm into elbowing my phone to my face. I stare at it with all the jaded focus at my disposal and I eke out gets a 'thanks' and smiley. I'm not pining for more chat or any social gathering. I'm finding it incapable of answering phone calls or texts. I'm moping inside my bedsit, in my bed and inside my skin. But Fiona's idea of revenge swarms my mind. Facebook stalking thrills me in waves ebbed away with sober realisation of its pointlessness. But I know I spent four years being cautious. The negatives are swelling my mind as if already becoming obstacles. All I want is to make him pay, to make her pay. Someone is paying me back. I doze off.

*****

Why didn't I see this coming? I could have gone through Jon's pockets, or rummaged around his flat looking for suspicious scents or underwear. I should have kept a running tally of his nights away, and checked his Facebook for notifications and messages from girls. There was a secret life which I had never suspected. Even his posts were suspicious by their lack of updates, still the same old background photo of his car. I search through old emails, and get sucked into old chains where I came across as the non-committal one. I'm feeling furious remembering all the times in the first months when he said he loved me and I never said it back. I log back into Facebook and scroll up and down with abandon. He has changed his favourite songs list and unsubscribed from the *Massive Attack* page. It's a message for me. I click on Friends of friends until I reach the mythical six degrees of separation. There's a Gary with a handsome face I add in some impulsive act of revenge.

Then I go back to the Other Woman.

She looks classy, porcelain pale, like a ballerina with a feather stuck up her stupid butt. I'm sure bluebirds flap over her hair when she gets up in the morning. I take a second look at her ridiculously long lashes. Her body flows where everything else in her IKEA bubble contracts. Her pine table screams minimalist. Her facial cream pic catches the probably fake plant in the corner of her bathroom perfectly, along with a shiny rectangular showerhead. Her square-shaped jets of water offer some rejuvenating qualities that my limescaled roundhead lacks. Her sleek white rug never stains from the Barrolo wine she ironically flaunts as her Lidl conquest. As if this bitch ever goes to discount supermarkets for real. Then the London posts are all wrong. Too much natural light. It looks like she's standing in a beam at Greenwich observatory. *This place is paradise,* she posted, attracting a dozen likes and hearts already.

Well, paradise ain't paradise for everyone bitch.

I take a swig of Chardonnay and my body warms immediately as I flap the laptop down. It's no use. I open it again. I try to focus on the Reddit page about surviving affairs. The well-meaning posts punctuate my swills of wine. *Just stay positive. Keep healthy and focus on yourself. Get your paperwork and bank details in order, in case he behaves like a dick. Don't rush into any rebound relationships.* It's no good. I log onto Facebook again. This bitch is a virtual catwalk model. I bet her farts smell like lavender. Me, I'm invisible. I'm a twenty-eight-year-old nobody stuck in the same job for five years. None of my colleagues who started with me are here any more. I'm on my fifth manager. Now they've started being appointed younger than me. The last one rolled her eyes at me the other day when I jammed the Nespresso machine with some generic coffee pods.

Fuck it. I kick my jeans down to my ankles and stretch out on my bed. I give up on the laptop and don't check texts. The bed feels huge now. I shuffle across from my usual left side to the middle, but it doesn't feel right. A burglar alarm goes off somewhere down the road. A bus chunders past. My neighbour upstairs is taking ages using her electric toothbrush or the world's loudest vibrator. I pull the cool duvet around me and press my head into my pillow.

*****

I take the bus to town. Now would be the time to visit my parents in Leicestershire. Aren't jilted women supposed to? It can't be worse than the pitying looks I get from married friends when I leave London for a week over Christmas to spend time vaguely with family. I could listen to my mother saying men are all the same and commenting on my London swagger while dad makes himself scarce mowing the lawn. But I don't want to burden them with the sight of their only child dumping her woes on their humdrum lives. I can only manage a day at theirs. Spending the night became impossible after I turned about 25. I can't bear my mum fretting over how I refuse to fill up the dishwasher before switching it on, or dad's annoying vanishing acts to the shed. They're house-rich working-class Tories who make it their business to look down on other working-class people just because they're common. Needless to remember, they fawned over Jon. They have no interesting pictures on the walls, only still life and fruit. Television volume turned down and the same dreary repertoire of afternoon viewing. I don't want to retreat to my childhood bedroom and stare at the faded Leonardo di Caprio *Beach* poster on the room door. A weekly call reassuring them

I haven't got stabbed or raped on my way home to the estate is enough.

Each shop and café on the high street looms as a flashback indicting my happy times with Jon. All the landmarks look the same as back then, even though everything else has suddenly changed. The bus stop where he melted me with the chat-up line *What would you like to do, if you were free of any consequences*, spitting ashes now. The pub where he first snogged me, drunk enough not to notice that I had heaved up in the alley a few minutes before, the club where he introduced me to Massive Attack in the chillout room, then the WHSmith where he lost both our renewed passports the day before we flew on our first holiday together to Italy: it all trundles in my gut along with the wheels on the potholes. The bus stops at the pelican crossing. A man looking like my ex stands smiling. I want to pinch myself. His smile is followed by a little wave as his partner stands behind a pushchair in the middle of the crossing. I gulp. In my mind's eye a lost dream of parenthood vanishes. I press my elbow onto the window ledge as the bus takes me home.

I want to withdraw fifty outside the Costcutter but my card is returned on my first attempt. I check my balance and feel sick. £21 left until the day after tomorrow. Rent, travel card, and credit card have all screwed me. I'm lucky to have missed university top-up fees by a year or I would have that draining my account, too. I get some marked-down bananas, and cherry tomatoes to fend off scurvy.

When I get home I scroll through Jon's messages and his lover's posts for the millionth time. Poking around bitchface's media is wrong, I know. Her name is Hoi. To me that sounds too trite. Bitchface is more appropriate. Lifting the lid afresh sends a shiver down my spine. She's posted an infuriating selfie with Jon at the edge with his blond stubble and dimple chin revealing he is smiling. He might at least have displayed a taught jawline, as if proving that he's unhappy and regretful and plotting his way back to me. Why do men use their power to walk out on a woman, only to surrender it again like a puppy dog to this fake beauty? She is infuriatingly international, with gay-looking contacts in Hong Kong, patrician blondes from the mid-west of the US, and windswept-looking outdoorsy guys in the UK. She has lots of male contacts but keeps the women decently in the majority. I switch to Jon and click on his recent pics with her. Self-flagellation feels good with a glass of wine in your other hand. Jon's affair did not break my world. It just made everything strange. Nothing I could see in my flat seemed real any more, as if the whole promise of living together had been a fraud from the start. Most days I'm fine and don't think too hard about it. I'm good at not dwelling on trauma. I'll be fine.

Jon's pared-back images exert some treacherous glamour over me. It's as if I'm expecting something to jump out. He always had mysterious allure, akin to an elegant woman with a naturally attractive face even when unmade-up in the morning. His pics exude an ill-deserved confidence. I bet my bank account, all £14 of it, that she is using him. I scroll down to the first pic where bitchface commented. When I click the *Something went wrong* message takes over my screen. I go back and the screen doesn't change. The bastard's blocked me, like in the time it took me to refill my glass. I breathe out staggered. I check the text from Fiona: *no update hun x*. I try Linkedin. I haven't bothered with it for ages but I find his name. His profile pic is new. He is wearing a white shirt and red tie, but his face becomes pixellated as I zoom in on it. I can't remember my password. But not logging in means he can't trace me. I set up a fake Linkedin and get a contact pending. Then I do the same with a couple of Facebook accounts, processing 'Alice' and 'Ellie' as grey pages so I can check out Jon's profile.

I stay in the Alice account and search for Jon. I'm channelling my inner Fiona. But I'm not being vague and demure. I'm going to hit him with suspenseful nod to my best friend's Skype activities: *If it's you I'm sorry for kicking off last night*. My message remains on 'Sent'. I add him,

CATFISH HONEYTRAP

too. My mind is entering an emotional post-mortem. If Jon accepts Alice's add, it means bitchface isn't special. If he messages back I have leverage.

    I collate all the letters, cards and photos I've got from him. They're brilliantly young, from the time before he got a digital camera. The lilac walls of his mother's cottage, the first wristband he made me, theatre receipts from our dates, and a collage of I Love You cuttings taken from random letters from *Loaded* and the *NME*. I stuff it all away in two shoeboxes, like a museum replica of a lost youth, or a stash of incriminating evidence, as if I can sit down with a glass and piece together bit by bit a chronology of what went wrong. I push the boxes under the pillow end of my bed. Having them close when I sleep will aid my dreams for revenge. If only he could ghost me for real. A widow's life would give me dignity and a dozen variations of sob stories to pawn off.

Chapter 2

'We're going out hun!'.

I was thinking tonight would be a quiet one of Facebook lurking and *Grand Designs* on TV. But my best friend is dragging me out. Fiona uses the same tone as when she lectures about the need to move to Richmond, as if it's just a question of being close to Heathrow and seven-figure house prices are a mere trifle compared to fuss-free flights to New York. She is hovering over the doorframe, facing Her Only Single Friend, and new project. She has a smart formal after-office look and won't wait around for me to look stunning.

'I'm fine, really.' But to be honest the prospect of going out for a few hours would stall another evening of dwelling on Jon's absence from my life.

'Oh my god. You just said *fine*. You must really be feeling shit'. She sits on the end of my bed, gesturing me to get ready. 'It's Lola's birthday. Just the pub on the corner, come on'.

'Nah, you got without me'.

'Come on, hun. You could do with getting out. It can't do much good staying in watching *The Stabbing*'.

'*The Killing*'.

'Exactly. Seriously Faye, come on'.

Fiona loves me but she leeches on me emotionally in the way only a better-off female friend can. Her eyes shine with glee noticing how I'm the reliable loser she knew before Jon was in the picture. My fuck-up probably makes her feel good about her Marketing job, her new media lifestyle, her weird fiancé in New York obsessed with virtual sex. But I don't want to stay shipwrecked on the desert island of my bed, feeling sorry for myself and getting maudlin over Jon.

I rummage around in my drawer, looking for something nicer that still fits. Nothing looks right so I smooth the dress down that I'm wearing, ignoring the rawness of my razor burn exacerbated by today's heat and movements. I'm going without foundation. I feel very monochrome in my plain grey outfit and trainers. Maybe Fiona's long-term monogamy with a man who spends half his time in the US means I am now her sudden link to the world of singledom. She should be wanting me to join her, in the same way she wanted me to find a flat on her posh side of the road, innocent of such concepts as deposits and guarantors. She should be praising the joy of Skype in bonding a relationship, right down to the freaky things her man likes to do with her online. But there's no sign. She's brisk in snatching this singlehood liberty. I feel she wants to link arms with me as we enter the pub.

'He's an idiot, Faye. He'll never get to know what he's missing out on', Lola says, giving me a sweaty hug. I'm not used to hugging. It doesn't come naturally to me and now there's no man hug any more. Lola's aged since I last saw her. Her skin shows traces of a faded tan that makes her face look sallow. She's delightfully pissed already. That spares any boring smalltalk.

'Yeah some Hong Kong woman he was chatting to online for ages', Fiona chips in. The other women take a second to absorb my loss, then go 'aaaw' in unison. I sigh as I tilt the pint glass to my lips.

'Oh that's shit babe. Got himself a Geisha girl', Lola blurts out. I'm pretty sure a geisha can only be Japanese. But I saw the film and the actress was Chinese. So I let the comment pass.

'She found out on his phone', Fiona added.

'Jeez, it sucks but well done you on being the detective. To think of all the affairs starting online screwing up people's lives'.

'Thanks', I smile as my nose starts to dip into the glass. I should be drunker. I'm never good at smiling. I should practise in front of the mirror for a natural look, not the chimp-like grimace I can barely hide with my glass. And I'm hopeless with all these privately-educated, creative wankers.

'Hey you should set up a detective agency, help other women like you'.

'Or make him jealous, hun'. Fiona has almost finished her pint in silent listening. 'Take some pics of you with the guys here and post them on Facebook. That'll prick his ego'.

I do deserve his regret. The least he could do would be to sniff around my Facebook posts, seeing how happy I am without him.

'Get under someone to get over someone girl', Lola cackles. 'Get someone exciting. Jon sounds so, you know, *mediocre*'.

I let my smile loose and allow my pint glass to angle several degrees indecently as I down the rest. I would take back mediocrity tomorrow and wouldn't know what to do with excitement. Maybe she means Aaron. I don't know if Lola knows about the Skype shenanigans Fiona gets up to with her fiancé, so I refrain from making a joke. I look at the table behind Lola that's sitting four rugby types. They're wearing shiny shirts and wankerish shoes. One knocks a bottle to the floor when he juts his arms out making a punchline to some joke.

Fiona asks me to come to the loo with her. I want to talk to her about the detective idea. I've been standing in the conversation like a coiled spring. But she switches to something else, as if her mind's moved on, which it always does. I have to wait for the adjoining cubicle and as usual she never waits for me to finish.

'Catch you back in the bar hun'.

I hear sobs from the other loo next to me. I ask if the woman's OK. She says she met a guy and they added each other on Facebook. They hooked up last night and he said he would meet her in this pub. But he hasn't shown and now he's blocked her. I ask her to come out of the loo to talk properly. But she says half her make-up has run and she feels enough of an idiot already. There's a crack between where the separating panels meet the doors, so I tell her to peer through it. I see her huge green eye with an imploring look magnified by her spoiled mascara. The sound of Take That's *Flood* vibrates faintly through the cubicle and onto my pressed cheek.

CATFISH HONEYTRAP

'Fucker', she says. 'It felt like we were connecting, him adding me like that. I didn't get his fucking number or address and now he's just vanished into thin air'.

I tell her he's a fucker and give her an attagirl. I don't have the knack of making friends easily, and there's something liberating about connecting through the crack of a toilet door. I tell her I just got chucked for another woman. For some reason I tell her how I once had a panic attack at university when I had to sit still in a hoodie in a seminar for half an hour and managed not to be noticed. So her makeup catastrophe is nothing.

'Thanks', she snivels.

I should comfort her more but I want to get back to Fiona to talk about the Facebook idea. But when I join Fiona again with the others the conversation has switched. Lola's rattling through a story at whiplash speed. When she finishes I sit laughing at it, a story I haven't been listening to.

Some of Lola's friends show up. A burst of laughter surges from something Fiona says and I wonder what it is I've missed. Lola's hiding another giggle. The sight of her bracelet sliding down her clammy forearm sets off something in me.

'Wow, you're paying over a grand for a bedsit on that estate?', someone actually fucking called Elspeth asks me, as if I'm some council estate fetishist instead of being born ten years too late for the housing boom. I could protest that's it's not technically a bedsit, seeing as my tiny kitchen has a sofa. But I shuffle her off. I don't want her faghag vibes. There's no respite from her friend, who sees in my slumming a cue to waffle on about his sustainability project. Something about converting a load of used freight containers into carbon-neutral canalside housing.

*****

The next night is more of the same. I still can't believe I stayed out so late. So many guys at Fiona's work do and being pissed lowered all my inhbitions. For a natural introvert I'm surprisingly at home in indoor spaces full of people. Whenever I say anything in the office, it's as if my sound button is muted. But three pints at midnight and I'm the best of a bad bunch. We're all stranded in South London, in shit house-shares on mediocre salaries, all waiting for our futures to begin.

I used to get blackout drunk, sometimes waking up with my jeans down at my ankles. This time age conferred me the comfort of a taxi ride to my own flat. This morning I'm going to check my texts and email before the hangover sets in. There's an overturned wineglass by my crotch. I reach down for dampness but can't find any. At least I finished the Chardonnay before passing out. So many of those guys added me on MSN.

I remember about a dozen conversations with as many men. At least half were my widow fantasy. I can't remember how many times Jon had died in my pissed chats. There was the heart attack, the suicide, the Somali pirate attack, and the homecoming find on the toilet. The toilet was the best revenge. When Jon dumped me he had enough decency to do it face-to-face in a coffee shop rather than by text. After saying *I'm splitting up with you* I stifled a murmur and pretended I needed the toilet. It was one of those solitary unisex ones in a crowded place. There was probably a queue forming outside. But I just sat there, flanked by a graffiti dick and some Tory-bashing, as if waiting for Jon to stand up and tap apologetically on the door. Luckily I was probably not drunk enough to regale the random men with that depressing information. In any case my low-cut top would have stopped most of them from listening.

I didn't even remember uploading Facebook to my smartphone. But now awake with a dry mouth in bed I discover the bliss of scrolling. I seek them out and end up looking at their posts for an hour. It seems like a lot but I'm greenlighting them from the comfort of my mattress

CATFISH HONEYTRAP

instead of getting wasted enough to pass out somewhere. When Fiona texts me to check on me I ask her if this is normal. She says it's like dating on Match, and I should get used to it before I turn thirty, squiggly eye and LOL. *Believe in your wonderful self!* I smile. Those were her last pre-puke words after a night out in Barcelona last summer.

She was satisfyingly as fat as me then. I held her lovely hair and removed her heels as she vomited Jäger bombs down the toilet. I managed to drag her onto her bed, to lay her head aside her pillow, and to tell her everything was going to be fine: 'and you still look hot after you puke'. *No way, hun, you're waaaay hotter.* Now I'm scrolling through her Facebook posts and she's fat-tagged me in a pic next to her and Lola. Fiona has a genius of staging off-hand moments and making herself look iconic. Even at uni she had the knack of walking with me into a pub and immediately catching men's gazes like something magnetic. I sigh and switch to my DMs. Then I see a message from Gary. I don't remember him from last night. But I scroll down his posts and remember he was my random sixth separation add. A random *sup?* earns a *not much*. After five more text exchanges he sends a selfie from his bed and wants the same from me.

I log out, put my phone down, and drag out the shoeboxes again. Jon was real. His decision robbed me of my chance to confront him. *Why are you being a cheat and an arsehole?* would have elicited a tongue-tied response and some pleas for forgiveness. He robbed me not just of my happiness but of my chance to occupy the moral high ground. He's turned me into a stalker. Now the offline memory boxes can't be resuscitated any more than the online posts of the men who gave me their numbers can be fashioned into the perfect rebound. The weekend is young and I'm staying in. I'm taking Fiona's advice. We live in a world of internet dating. I'm setting up a Match account. Just not one of me.

Bitchface's pouty Facebook pics are so easy to slut out. Setting up a Hoi account takes no time. *Remember a truthful photo with a great profile goes a long way!*. Well, there's sincerity in my faking. Her latest Facebook pic with her airhead smile and the cocked Barrolo bottle at her cheek sums up her frilliness rather well. I leave her age preferences from 20 to 60. I think of writing a desperate bio but can't seem to make anything sound real. Instead I scroll through random men listed as living in the same borough as Jon, clicking *Interested* at everyone with a pulse and some wood. I try to locate his workplace too, but Match won't let me narrow down the search. No matter. Sooner or later she'll get found out.

I leave the bitchface profile online and try drafting my own account.

Profile name: Faye Gardner. ~~Should I give out a fake name?~~
Age: 28. ~~Lie?~~
Area: ~~Shithole in Croydon~~. South London (sounds hipster).
Occupation: ~~Student~~. I wish.
Bio: ~~OCD jiltee with trust issues~~. Single professional woman about to live her best life.

Urrrgh. I google dating profiles but lose patience scrolling through cheesy advice about concentrating on being young, beautiful and engaging. The sample male dating bios restore my faith in human frailty. Publishing, sales execs and e-commerce galore. Not a single sewer worker or call-centre operative in sight. Not sure what an 'entrepreneur' is supposed to mean. *Inception* as favourite film at least twice. A middle-aged man listing 20% hearing loss in his left ear is a new one on me. The women profiles are full of homemakers and fulltime mums. Obviously not that full-time with all these entrepreneurs in their DMs. The pouty women are hiding their fat bodies with overhead selfies. I love the spread of tatted obese women for their fuckyou vibes and the comparative boost to my own chances.

After some more swigs I play around with profiles. Who wants to be me when they could be someone else? I find some of the Match women on their Facebook accounts. They should catfish some of their betterlooking friends to get a sales exec rather than an e-commerce guy playing computer games in his parental home. I don't see why I should expose myself with normal pics, and then get my chubby defectiveness told back to me. I also don't want to cheat like the others by posting twenty-two-year-old pics of myself. I delete my Match profile. Whatever I'm going to do now, it's not going to be online dating.

Bitchface Hoi can take all the flak on my behalf. Besides, it's been a few days and Jon has finally replied to 'Alice'.

Sorry you got the wrong Jon. I know an Alice from work so I accepted the request. I hope you find the right one.

He is 'Active'. There's no time like the present.

'Sorry no I met this guy with your name on internet dating and we had a chat over video call and I lost it and told him to pretty much fuck himself. I'm so sorry x.'

My reply is seen right away. The dots indicate my ex is replying.

Fair enough. All is fair in love and war and all that.

'Maybe I'm too overwhelming I don't know lol'.

More dots. This is like communicating with a ghost. A man dead to me is alive to this fake 'Alice' in an unknown form. Even in the formal and assured way he writes I recognise Jon's style.

Maybe? I'm a stranger so I can't say. But video chat is a tricky one for dating I think.

'Yes I'm a idiot it's not really like me to do that and he was just wanting all sorts of sleazy stuff so I kicked off whoops lol'.

I'm plagiarising Fiona and definitely overdoing it. What sort of woman chats like this to a stranger? I should delete my message. But before I decide Jon has seen it and the dots reappear.

Sorry you said you confused him with me?

'Yeah lol'. I'm clenching my stomach, trying to keep my feelings under control with this relationship ghost.

His name was Toogood? And you only set up this Facebook account last week.

'Yeah that's right'.

This person is not contactable on Messenger.

I exhale with a nervous murmur. I swallow heavily. The saliva was building up in my mouth. Block me once, shame on you. Block me twice ... I scroll down the homepage of the Yahoo search engine. I'm controlling the trembling in my hand. News glazes over my eyes. Austerity hammering local authority budgets, some Hollywood actor dating a woman half his age, a new film, violence in the Arab world. I type 'should I be a catfish?' in the search-bar. The transspecies ambiguity of the request puzzles the search results. I get a link about cod fishing in the Atlantic and another about a new film. 'Should I be a PI?' yields me a solid list of blogposts and links.

Hypothesis: When in doubt, ask a friend in the know.

I text Fiona: 'that thing Lola said when she was pissed, about being a private investigator'

Yeah?

'I want to do it'.

Sorry do what? Detective work?

'Yeah, what do you think?'

Outstanding. Just don't get dildo-bombing any more estate agents hun lol

It's been almost a week since my sleuth visit and there's no inkling of the collapse in the relationship that I've been obsessing over. No tearful posts from Hoi complaining about Jon dumping her. No text from Jon telling me that she's gone psycho or that she's been cheating and how stupid he feels. No plea to get back with me. There's not even any message from the estate agent asking if I'm missing a dildo. Not that they would know who to contact anyway. I called as Joanne Thompson from my untraceable work landline. I'm not sure what I should expect, but silence does not seem right. I'm setting up a fake Facebook account as 'Joanne Thompson', adding Streatham to her bio because I told the beady-eyed estate agent I had a property to sell there. When I called the agency to arrange the viewing I could hear the woman on the other end taking notes. She must have 'Joanne' on file somewhere. After the new Facebook profile gets approved the first thing I do is add a like on the estate agent's page. I'm a good catfish citizen now.

Chapter 3

It's been three days since I left the void of scrolling and cyberstalking. I wonder how agoraphobia develops, and whether it might be infecting me. I have traversed spacetime where my lived experience suddenly became a lie. That spacetime chugged along without me, while everyone and everything else I've even known carried on regardless. The colossal chasm of grief felt worse than death. Death is a final punctuation to a life and relationship truly lived. But an affair of lies is months of pulverizing stomach punches delivered in a compressed dose after the fact. I still feel lonely, as if on my deathbed. I can't access Jon's Facebook. And Fiona says Hoi has still not accepted her add. Jon's Linkedin is still live. I enlarge his face so it fills my laptop screen. Then I log out, feeling queasy at my obsession. I never heeded Fiona's advice. I should have spent my mid-twenties getting as much cock as I wanted.

As a woman you only get one youth. Jon wasted mine.

But I'm not going gently into the good night. I'm taking revenge. Nobody could imagine my calm genius as I stand outside the PC World on the Old Kent Road. I am carrying two brand-new laptops and watching dozens of future clients go about their business. Everymen shuffle past: fathers dragging reluctant kids, families fitting out a new home, thirty-something handymen bearing muscles and multiple women on speed-dial. I wonder how many people live like this, edging work one day to the next, living from wage to wage, clutching garden furniture with the same ritualistic joy of religious gatherings of old.

The wonder of my plan is mocked by the dreary routine of my day job.

You could walk past my office-block without giving it a second thought. It looks like every other one in the area. Ours is a little grubbier. It's a hairshirt for local authority cuts. I have the lift to myself because I'm late. I don't mind sharing the journey to the eighth floor with other people. Even though it gets full, nobody is really present.

CATFISH HONEYTRAP

Everyone's mind is elsewhere, worrying about a passive-aggressive remark, remembering to send a chase-the-chaser email, wondering if they forgot their packed lunch. And these elsewheres get to flank me as I walk to my desk. I blend into the scenery. It's an anonymous version of Jon egging me on during the hike in Italy four years back. He said I could burn off my body weight of pizza and gnocchi. At the peak above Lake Como he showed me the Madonna at the Ghisallo Pass. It represents the agony and joy of climbing a mountain, and the two figures in the sculpture are collapsed in each other's arms.

But now I'm walking by myself, with nobody to occupy my awkwardness or block the stares. I get more looks than usual. They make me feel as though I'm radioactive and about to sprinkle polonium in the coffee machine. Then I remember that I have to give a presentation. I'm so nervous that I pour too much milk in my coffee. My mind is elsewhere and it's my turn to present on the social media marketing strategy. I left a memory stick of my slides in the store room. When I get there Harry has his hands full of folders. To keep the door open he stands in front of it, making me have to brush past him to go through. I breathe in sharply. There's a gormless smile on his face, something between smarmy and sexual. The shelf where I thought I left the data is now bare. I take a quick survey of the other shelves but can't see my USB anywhere. I know I've saved ten Powerpoint slides in Q drive. But when I get back to the lectern I see that the new line manager has logged out before dashing off for another strategy meeting. Not to worry. I log in using my own ID.

'How can we improve our social media profile?', I blurt out to my twodozen colleagues occupying half the seats in front of me. They don't look happy congregating and have drawn out the chairs at weird angles and are sitting on them a few paces apart, as if wanting to guard against being lectured. I would prefer them lined up as a bloc. I hate public speaking and I get triggered by people doing their own thing when they're supposed to be listening.

'Facebook, Twitter, Linkedin? I'm all ears'. I smile without thinking. There's no reply. I look towards Aparajita. She's normally supportive in her peculiarly middle-aged way, but even she's not moved to speak out of sympathy. She just looks down at her Ipad as if I'm a ghost.

'OK, well let's think about that while I log into my presentation'. I log in with my password and switch on the projector. There's a few seconds of emptiness on the screen behind me. There's no projection. It's not connected for some reason. I switch various buttons on and off on the control panel but nothing changes. I fiddle with the mouse and switch the monitor on and off. My fiddling gets more panicked. I smile awkwardly at my audience, none of whom respond in kind. 'Sorry there's something wrong with the projection'.

'It was working fine earlier', Aparajita says, probably thinking she is being helpful.

She makes her vowels work hard whenever she speaks. There's a sigh from the back. Then some murmuring that flows forward into a general chatter. Eventually Tim the IT man comes to the rescue. My anxiety ebbs until I realise that Tim's fiddling exposes me to a minute of staring at my bemused colleagues. My smile opens at them again and I mumble an apology. Finally Tim fixes it and takes his leave with a thumbs up. I labour through my talk which I have just managed to make awkward as well as boring.

Later I take a longer lunch break and eat at my cubicle where no-one will mind if I don't talk. I google 'how to be a private investigator', typing as quickly as I lose patience with the answers. I scroll through webpages on my office computer. But they're too dense. Besides, I have a best friend who encouraged me in this, and she knows men who know websites. And I know the vibe. Sex, the promise of sex, entraps men. And the power of social media is glaring at me. So many times Fiona has told me about Aaron's Skype sex, getting off when she tells him to spank his arse and when he tells her to turn

CATFISH HONEYTRAP

random vegetables from the fridge into sex toys. I'm not even going to use Lurpak as a lubricant and I'm going to get paid instead of some vague promise of marriage.

I log into Facebook and see a message from Gary: *you're hot x*. A whole cyberworld of business lies at my fingertips. I scroll down Gary's posts. There's one of him on a sun-lounger with a blonde-haired woman leaning on his shoulder. Another of him sitting with friends in a football pub. I press my jaw into my right palm, scrolling, and thinking of a way into all these potential relationship breakdowns.

'Who's that?'. Harry asks me before rearing into his chair next to me.

'New boyfriend already?'

I give a nervous laugh. I shove the keyboard so hard my desk shakes. Harry sits down with gasping laugh of his own. For a man with no sense of humour he finds himself hilarious. He flips a page across his keyboard with an unwanted grace and starts typing. His hair is in a lopsisded slant revealing he didn't comb it after getting out of bed. I stare to the left at my phone, pretending some friends have texted me, even though they haven't. Then I sneak a sideways glance at him, only to see him doing the same back to me.

'Thanks Faye. Have you got a sec?'

It's Aparajita's trilly voice. A sec? No, not really Aparajita. My body has gone stiff and my heart is palpitating. I didn't hear her approach from behind and she might have seen on my screen what Harry just missed.

'Sure, no probs. Just let me save the school regeneration file'.

Aparajita smiles and walks to her office. The man from Health and Safety is in today. He's wandering down the entrance corridor unwedging fire-resistant doors and wheeling out chairs to check whether they can take out a child's finger or something. If he pulls this stunt at a hundred different workplaces he could be in contact with thousands of strangers each day. Shame he's such a jobsworth that colleagues would rather swerve into one of my social media feedback sessions than run the risk of being lectured by him. My mind continues to dwell on this meandering man while Aparajita suggests teaming up with someone else to share the social media strategy. I tell her I think I'll be fine but will let her know.

*****

The bus ride back into Croydon fills me with an unknown inspiration. Aparajita offered to put me back on grants or to job-share the social media strategy. She said it in a casual way that did not sound like a bollocking for wasting company time chatting to Gary. But I'm keeping the role. I'm piggy-backing the job for freelance. As I alight near my flat I feel the first sense of after-work elation in about four years. Even the homeless man who always sits on the grass opposite my stop seems to smile in anticipation. The sunny warmth layers a feeling of luxury on top of my new freedom. It's hot enough not to be uncomfortable, but enough to get me flecked with sweat as I enter my four-storey housing block.

When I get home I answer Fiona's texts about Aaron.
'Still no bitchface accept?'
Nah, sorry hun x.
'Sucks. Well I've set up some fake accounts anyway.'
Go girl. You got stalking rights lol
'Lol. How's Loverboy doing? You said he's got into Tai Chi?'
Yeah
'He's going to do that in New York?'
Pretty bad, right?
'You getting worried?'
Yeah. Do me a favour hun.
'OK'
Those fake accounts you're building. Add Aaron on a few of them. Let me know if he replies.

CATFISH HONEYTRAP

'Sneaky, but yeah no worries'.
Sneaky and bad. He's making me bad the fucker.
Not as bad as what I'm doing. I log into bitchface Hoi's Match account and there's a manoswamp of messages in her inbox. After reading through the first few the repetition of *hey babys* and lame jokes makes my eyes glaze over. There's one called Zak, a hairdresser who looks a bit like Jon, whose idea of a chat-up line is *I always burn my rice. Fancy showing me how it's done? x.* I reply with lame emojis and lols without even reading the messages. But what am I supposed to do next? I'm almost certain where she lives now because I checked Jon's phone way back before I confronted him. He had a text asking for advice about a strange address. I made a note of it. But I can't bring myself to give out her actual details to these strange men. I'm not done with Hoi but I'm not going to let her get stalked and harassed by all these entrepreneurs and *hey babys*. I limit my responses 'add me here on Facebook.' I copy her address to about thirty of the passably handsome men, as well as an older Chinese man called Qiang Yu. Likes and hearts on her posts from random men should make Jon see sense.

*****

It turns out my 2:1 in Criminology is going to pay the bills after all. My website is ready. I used a random PI site as a template. Fiona's a darling for doing the posh voice answer-message and a couple of fake testimonials. The local Costa is buzzing with people who seem to have ducked in to avoid the sudden downpour. Still Fiona manages to find us a spot at the counter. I show her the webpage I printed out at the office. She plops her new I-phone down. It's the same model as mine. It's nice to see her follow my trend for once. But rather than typing on my screen I pull out some notepaper. I scribble on it to check my pen was working. But then my nose tells me Fiona won't be offering notes. She reeks of stale vodka and old cigarettes. I press my nose into my upturned palm and breathe through my mouth. She beams over the document and downs a shot of Espresso as if it's a tequila.

'Has Aaron left for New York?'

'Yeah'. Her tone is flat.

'Oh. What happened to your romantic send-off?'

'He massaged my feet with a cold Pellegrino'. She jolts her cup into the saucer with a ceramic clunk. 'At the Heathrow Hilton no less.'

I snort into my cappuccino. Her deadpan gets me every time.

'I got blisters from the half-marathon. It felt nice to be fair. Seriously, we used to do it constantly. That amazing waking up sex. Now he's all into texting and Skyping'.

'I don't know. A cold can on blisters sounds OK to me'.

Fiona eyerolls and smiles. A low chuckle slips from her throat.

'Anyway, speaking of the internet, what did your friend say?'

'Oh, just the usual, I suppose. Encryption, don't use dumb security passwords, watch out for phishing, that sort of thing'.

She gives me a conspiratorial look.

'He doesn't know what you're really going to do. What were the profiles you set up?'

'Oh, Ellie Carr and Alice Long', I reply sipping my coffee. Fiona deftly logs into her phone and starts typing.

'Found them hun. Just liked Alice's profile pic. Not being funny but she looks fake, the Ellie one, too'.

Well, *durgh*, I only created them last week and haven't touched them since.

'I just shared an IKEA page with Alice. Random traffic like that makes her look more convincing'. IKEA takes me right back to bitchface. Fiona upturns the remains of the Espresso in her mouth and pulls her handbag onto her shoulder.

'Well what about the Ellie one?'

'Fuck's sake hun it's all fake, who cares?'

'Well if it's fake, let me use you for the Ellie profile pic'.

'Are you freaking mental?.' Fiona smiles as she reaches for the emptied espresso cup on the counter.

'Not a face face, just a crazy one with you waving your hair. I'll make it crazy Ellie'.

Without a moment's hesitation Fiona's eyes light up. She flaps her hair around like we're doing a music video. I take a couple of pics.

'Nice. OK, I'll upload this one. You're all hair and no face'.

'OK mentaloid. Have fun. Gotta dash now hun'.

I take five minutes to finish my own coffee and make my way to the bus stop. The warm rain is hammering hard. It continues even as the sun comes out and the wet smell is gorgeous after the stale air in the café. I look at the blotted scribbles in the notepaper in my hand. The rainwater is turning it into dregs like old tea. When I get home I breathe in deep, filling my lungs to elation. As I breathe out slowly, I speak a few prayer-like words in my head and I click on the website link in Fiona's email.

Here at Parsnip Investigations, we are proud to be your private investigators offering our expert surveillance and private investigation services in London, and the Home Counties. We offer you that personable touch most other London private detectives cannot. We pride ourselves with our professionalism and cost-effective solutions to any enquiry we receive.

Our expert London private investigation team have experience in investigations and surveillance. You are in safe hands. We use the latest technology from cameras to social media tracking devices to give you the best, cost-effective private investigation work.

The types of surveillance we conduct are: –

- *Domestic/Matrimonial disputes (such as affairs or cheating partners).*

- *Insurance Fraud Investigations, for example fraudulent claims*

- *Employee monitoring such as moonlighting, and any other surveillance requested on employees/directors.*

Any evidence we gather will be presented with reference to legal standards.

The second three are bollocks. I have no talent for those things, or any interest. I'm not even going to do the first one for real. Parsnip is all about honeytraps. Catfishing. Blackmail. Coercion. Extortion. I lay down for an early night, indulging my new bedtime ritual of scrolling through my newsfeed and checking on old friends and acquaintances. There are random profiles from school of people I never really knew, getting engaged or married, going on holiday together. Some are the usual suspects posting predictable stuff. Some older men I used to have crushes on now look bloated and pathetic in middle age. Others have not posted anything since begrudgingly opening their accounts a year or so ago. These remain exactly as I left them. What's the point of shunning social media? They're all friends of friends and will get photographed and posted whether they like it or not. I need to find a way to add catfish accounts to my phone. But I'm ready anyway. Three laptops sit on my desk where TV remotes and Kleenex used to be. The three models sit in peaking alignment, with Jon's main device in the middle flanked by two smaller computers. They are the only neat and orderly parts of my chaotic bedsit.

The next day Fiona asks me to join her down in Brighton for her friend's thirtieth. She wanted her to stay over for a dinner out with a single male friend of a friend. It's sweet of her but I know a better rebound. I go anyway. I've just set up half a dozen fake accounts and could do with some sea air. I need some real-world inspiration for name choices. I keep coming up with dated names like Emmas, Annes and Emilys, like I'm outlining a Jane Austen fanfic rather than a regional catfish empire.

CATFISH HONEYTRAP

I'm in an overheated carriage with a thirty-something businesswoman next to me. She has two folders, computer and a bag crammed under the seat in front of her. She is shutting down her laptop and starting the delicate standing manoeuvre, probably in search of a free toilet.

'Sorry, could you save this seat for me?'

She has the aloof air of an executive, used to getting her requests agreed. She doubtless thinks she's stooping enough already having to take an overcrowded train down to her pad in the South Downs or wherever. Part of me wants to say *keep your own seat safe you arrogant woman*. But I clock something interesting in her folders and don't cause a stink.

'Sure, toilet is it?'

She smiles and flits her skinny body past standing passengers down the passageway. Nobody is showing the least interest in our brief conversation. I take my chance. I put her folder on my lap and flick through the pages. There are photo IDs of dozens of people. They're mostly men. They all look old. Maybe they're wealthy shareholders in Mezzanine financial services. I pick up my phone and take eleven photos of the pages in all. There are probably more in her other folder but I sense my time is running out. Safe in the knowledge that I have at least a hundred new candidates for extortion I flop the folder back down and press my face into the passenger window. As the haughty woman returns she doesn't even acknowledge my favour with a smile, or even any eye-contact. She presses both folders together and puts them on the floor at her feet. My guilty mind sees suspicion in that act. But then she opens her laptop again and perches forward to type. Comfort made her do that rather than wariness at the catfish freak sitting next to her.

When I arrive in Brighton I find the others are already at the bar. The bar stool is the only uncomfortable backless one so I'm standing and politely nodding along to Jake's talk while everyone sits comfortably. Fiona rescues me from boredom by thrusting her device in front of my face.

'He says I'm being *demanding* of him. What should I say back?'

I rub my eyes and reach for the phone. But Fiona does not give it to me but holds it so I can see it from a distance.

'I can't see his text'.

She moves the phone closer. Aaron's text says he's saying he's jetlagged and can't just drop everything and chat with no notice.

'Just ignore him, Fiona. Give it a day and let him text you first'.

'He said he was going to call me on the train down. And I told him there's a rail strike. I had to stand as far as Hayward's Heath and he still couldn't be arsed. Fucker.'

She leans back into her seat and cradles her phone in two hands like a rare bird-egg.

'Faye, can you message him from one of your accounts?'

I pick up my phone and log into Alice.

'Just going to say *hey* alright?,' I say as I scroll to Aaron and jab the online keyboard.

I take a swill of the Peroni and receive Jake's inevitable conversation again. Strange how my Jon trauma's vanished from Fiona's mind but her six-figure Anglo-American fiancé's bro time with *Grand Theft Auto* is a source of consternation.

Ping!

There's a momentary stunned look in Fiona's face. One of us has been texted a few seconds after my *hey x*. But the sound came from her phone.

'See?'. Fiona shows me a wink from Aaron. 'An hour on my own coming down here and that's all I get.'

She retreats to her screen and Jake scans the bar, looking for some inspiration for a new line of conversation. I take this moment to open the pics I took from the train. There's photo after photo assembled in five rows per page. In any other scenario these grainy mugshots would look like a line-up, like the *Leicester Mercury* detailing the prison sentences handed down to the worst local burglars, rapists and armed robbers of the year two thousand whatever. I try to expand the images with my finger and thumb but they're too grainy. These juicy catfish targets will have to wait for closer inspection.

'Shit has he replied hun?'

Fiona's question reminds me that I'm spending a suspiciously long time squinting at the photos of complete strangers.

'No, I'm just double-checking. Nothing to worry about'.

'Cool. Drink up we're off to Horatio's next'.

When we find an outside sofa seat, Fiona and I sit down in unison and stretch out of legs in a groan. The combination of overcrowded strike strains and high-stepped barstools have taken their toll on our personal space. The cocktails are in disposable cups so we can take a stroll. But the wind is picking up. After accompanying them on the pier and getting molested by the din of crashing waves and some screaming kids, I make my excuses and leave. I give Jake my number anyway, just to fend off his puppy-eyed gawkiness and as a favour for Fiona. As the London-bound train takes me north through the mackerel-sky dusk I feel fired up by a sense of mission. I try enlarging the photos from the finance woman's folder and they're not any clearer in the lit-up train carriage than they were in the bar earlier. I log into Facebook and find a message request from a Megan I don't recognise. She's got a ridiculous blond ponytail, fake tan and nails encapsulating the smartphone in her selfie profile

You know him, she asks, attaching a profile pic of the random Gary bloke who messaged me last week.

'Why do you want to know?' My reply triggers an MSN response: *You can now call each other and see information such as Active Status and when you've read messages*. It's an automated message. But it seems to pass judgement on my brass neck.

Coz he's my boyfriend

'OK', I reply. I wait to see the telltale moving dots indicating she's typing. But there aren't any. 'We're just friends', I lie. I'm pretty sure random hungover texting and an offer a dick pic don't amount to friendship, even in the brave new world of social media.

Do u text him?

'Sometimes.'

Can you show me, if thats ok?

'OK, but he hasn't texted me in a while. Not since last week.' More dotless silence. But my message is seen. 'Do you want me to text you if he gets back in touch?'

This time the reply dots are taking ages. I'll arrive at London Bridge before she hits me with her essay of pleas or abuse.

'Yes plz. I think he's a cheater but I need evidence'. Two minutes it took her. I wonder what she deleted before she settled on that pithy statement.

'OK, I'll let you know. Don't add me as a friend or he might see'.

I make a mental note to send Megan a Parsnip Investigations advert after leaving her doubts to fester for a day or two. I put my phone back into my handbag and recline as the train pulls into Haywards Heath. An athletic man with a fold-up bicycle boards. He stacks it neatly and unwinds an Ipod cable before plugging it into his ear. Before he sits he gives me a smile. There's a knowing look in his eyes. There are trainloads full of Garys and Jons out here. If they're not cheating, it's on their minds. My sleuth job description is writing itself. I should be like a journalist. If there's no news, I'll make news. But I'm not dodgy dossiering my way into a war. Just making some money will be fine.

My phone vibrates and my mind is too lost to bother answering. I leave my phone on silent as nobody really beyond Fiona bothers contacting me anyway. After Ipod man can't comfortably take my gaze any more I sigh and pull out my phone. It's a voicemail, which strikes me as odd as Fiona knows my policy of hating voicemails. Maybe it's Megan mouthing off a piece of her mind after her texting composure.

CATFISH HONEYTRAP

But as I put the speaker part of the phone to my ear I realise it's Jake, being all keen and looking forward to hanging out again.

When I get home I find four emails in the Parsnip inbox. Two are spam and one is trying to sell me something. But one is genuine. Kerstin is engaged and her man is cheating. Interesting. I begin typing my reply. I have played out this message in my mind for days. But now something is stopping me clicking 'Send'. I feel the same sentiment as when I clutch an emptied Chardonnay glass, wanting a refill but with my conscience telling me not to take another sip. I think of a dozen 'what ifs'. What if Kerstin is as fake as me, or a plant set by Fiona's website friend. What if she's real but a time-waster? What if there's a union of private investigators I haven't heard about who are going to catch me out? I take a gulp of posh cider for courage before I remember it's the non-alcoholic one Jon used to get for me. I'm going to stall. I email to myself the file I photographed from the snooty woman.

Mezzanine finance. Outstanding male probate cases.

A row of elderly-looking dead men serenade my eyes. Nice work, idiot. What the hell. There's a Bartholomew Garner on the first page. Can't be too many Bartholomews knocking around any more. I search Facebook and find a memorial page to Bartholomew Garner, patron of the Cheshire Community Foundation. Sepsis at age 79 can't be a nice way to go. I scroll up and down the likes. There's one from a Mike Garner. He looks about 30, maybe a grandson. I add him before noticing it's my own account. Never mind. If he bites I'll pick him up with a catfish later.

Back to Parsnip. My brass neck stalking dead philanthropists emboldens me. My reply to Kerstin is hovering in draft form. I close my eyes and click 'Send' without looking. I have crossed the Rubicon blind.

Chapter 4

Catfishing is such a solitary activity. I don't think I have sat in silence for hours like this since my first year at high school when I would flop on the family sofa, chew dead-fly raisins, raise my feet on the sofa armrest, and caress clouds visible through the window with my toes whilst listening to the mantle clock tick away until my parents got home. My stomach grumbles. I reach into my handbag and pull out a half-eaten cereal bar. I unwrap it and raise it to my lips. But the smell puts me off, so I place it beside my mouse. I scroll through random Antonias, Heathers and Siobhans. I study their serious and fun-loving profiles like flashcards. I see their selfies from Australia, their bragging about dresses, their new futons and paid-off mortgages. Do these women who have the same height, same waist size, same wardrobes, have anything in common? Surely these things are the least interesting things to have in common.

I want to find women like me, absent-minded pushing thirties struggling with rent and dead-end jobs. But these yummy mummies, marketing managers and publishing executives allow me to get out of my own head. I adopt their personae without digging down into the details of their mental health issues, cheating partners, and wine o'clocks. Maybe I'm doing them a favour by stealing their posts and giving them their fifteen minutes of fame. Besides, you have no idea that your targets are really falling for it, or even if they're scamming you in return. It's not just that I don't know the rules. It's that I can't even ask anybody what they are. I now have a dozen fake accounts, ten women and two men for the moment I can work out what to do with the men. I rely on my intuition, and gradually accept the attrition of no bites, shit posts and hatefakers.

I remember reading Reddits about the erotic power of online relationships as a way of getting over a break-up. Now I see that sexuality plucked from the internet can be harnessed as a professional power. I'm not actually having sex at work, but I am exerting a charisma via the fakes that get enough men at my mercy to make up for the duds and no-shows. Jake is texting me and I find it hard to focus on the chance of a real-world relationship. He's a friend of Fiona so the stakes seem higher than they need to be.

Anyway, I had a relationship. Neither Jon nor bitchface have paid me back. Now I have the means to make them. I have thought about this email all week. I log into the Parsnip account and word Jon an email.

Dear Jon Toogood,

I hope you don't mind my reaching out to introduce myself. I'm the new Private Investigator at Parsnip Private Investigators. I'm representing the interests of Mr Qiang Yu who is planning to return to the UK soon to continue his business interests with Ms Cheung Hoi. We have been approached by him to ascertain the nature of your relationship to Ms Cheung Hoi.

Please be sure that any answer you give will be treated in confidentiality and we will pay you a fee of £100 for your information.

Anonymous sign-off. He blocked me but I don't remember him having any filter on stranger emails. I'll let that marinade. Fiona's coming over and I can check the Parsnip inbox later.

*****

'How's it going with Jake?', Fiona asks.

'Oh, not really my type to be honest', I reply sitting down at my desk. 'Still no reply from bitchface?'

'Nope'. She shows me her phone. The 'hi' she sent after the add remained unseen.

OK, well come and see what I've been doing with my fake accounts'.

'Are these all for real hun?' She scans each profile pic which I printed out at work.

'Yep'.
'OK, well, any replies?'
'That's only the tip of the iceberg honeypie'.
Fiona's eyes glaze over when I tell her I've created not just two but a dozen fake profiles. There's something petty in how she doesn't reply but instead pours herself a measly serving of Chardonnay. She leans over my shoulder to see the horny text poetry I've been summoning. My beautifully worded flirtations directed towards fully grown men are rewarded with a series of 'u xcited?,' 'banging' and 'cant wait 2 cu.'
'Any replies yet from Aaron?'
'Nope. Well I checked this morning. Let's have another look.'
I log into my three Aaron accounts and scroll through each chatbox. Alice's *hey x* from Brighton remains unseen. In fact there's not a single 'Seen' on any of them, let alone a reply.
'You're in the clear my dear'.
Fiona chews her bottom lip. The absence of any response to my honeytraps has created a new layer of uncertainty.
'He said we would Skype every day but there's something different about him now'.
'Different how?'
'Well, he keeps messaging but it's never convenient just to hang out together. I get lots of video calls from his office. But he's feeling all distant. Like not just three thousand miles distant'
I'm looking at her wanting to give her an *aaaw*. It feels nice turning the relationship problem tables on her, even if there's no real equality between us. Aaron is just being a bloke. Jon is gone for good.
'Anyway, how's the PI stuff coming along hun?.'
'Not bad at all. This one's Kevin, the one I told you about with the fetish'.
Her eyes do not reveal comprehension.
'The one with the arse fetish'.

'The alien one?'. Fiona knocks back the wine in one gulp. The look in her eyes suggests she's still thinking about Aaron's squeaky clean silence.

'Yeah, well it's a thing about using anal probes. Not just for backdoor action.'

'I get the picture, hun'. She is smirking. 'You should refer to him as ET Kevin. Make him sound like a superhero'.

Her phone pings. I see her forefingers flicking gently on her screen. I can't see the pictures. But I don't need to. Fiona's eyes have gone soft and smiling.

'Going to love you and leave you. Gym time for me'.

I return her smile as she leaves. She hasn't been to the gym since before the half-marathon. It's her Skype time with Aaron. A different kind of gym.

Now I'm on profile thirteen, Chloe or Claire, or some overweight people-pleaser name. I'll confirm it once I've finished filing away her bio. Claire is better. Fat Claire wants to be loved by everyone. She woos strangers and probably works as a PA, or care assistant. She once gave £20 to a beggar and annoyed her friend by sitting down with him to talk about life. On holiday in Morocco she was hopeless at haggling. She ended up paying ten pounds more than the gambit for a crappy necklace made out of fake pearls. The peroxide pics, endearing blue eyes and double chin were just right. I download six pics, post four, and keep two in reserve for the Claire file.

Meanwhile my Imogen account has been accepted by Kerstin's man, Chris. More of his posts are now visible. He looks like a beach bum in love with his muscly legs. I've thought about this ice-breaker. I know it's lame. But it's the best innocent pass I can imagine. Besides, Chris is one of those generic names. Chris is the definition of plausible deniability. There must be a few Chris driving instructors knocking about South London.

'Hi Chris. Thanks for accepting my add. I'm going to be free for driving lessons all weekends this month and the next x'.

*****

The next day there's an email from bitchface Hoi in my Parsnip inbox. *I don't appreciate your emails. Please do not contact my boyfriend again.* 'Boyfriend' doesn't stick in my craw as much as I feared. I take a shower and think about how to play this. Standing under a warm jet of shower declutters my mind. As I dry my hair I decide to turn it back onto her. Jon obviously showed her the email straight away. I'm going for broke. I word her an email in reply, hinting at Jon's infidelity. But after clicking 'Send', the email bounces back, marked undeliverable.

OK, bitch. I log into my Alice account to scroll up and down Hoi's posts. I spot some likes and hearts from men on her pics. But there were so many men in her Match account that I can't recall if these are the direct product of me advertising her Facebook profile in my multiple replies. I log into Match to check. There's probably a hundred more thirsty men with yellow fever in her inbox. Time for a hundred more replies of *Add me on Facebook here*. After entering the username and password a warning screen appears. *Your profile has been closed for suspicious behaviour. If you think this is an error, please contact the Customer Care team.*

Fuck.

If Fiona were looking over my shoulder she would call me a bunny boiler. But I won't give up. All that time and money Jon spent with her, he can pay back to me, somehow. He just won't know it. Until I work something out, I'll stick with Facebook. I'll model more accounts on her. I scroll through Hoi's recent posts, seeing how Jon's heart icons and pics are increasing. One of his pics must have been taken in a hotel bed because there are lightswitches on the headboard. Jon has added a public comment under a pic of him and her in Greenwich yesterday. *So happy to proclaim our love. No need for stalkers.* Stalker? I'm much more

CATFISH HONEYTRAP

than that. But if he thinks that's all I'm doing, I'm OK with it. I know how to hurt a man.

*****

I'm no longer anxious eating. I met Fiona for lunch the other day and we ordered an antipasti board. I let her eat all the meat and cheese while I chased the vegetables around with my fork. But now she's come to catch up on the catfishing, her plain talk is turning critical. After our usual chat about my shit job and her flaky fiancé we return to my new business model. She is scrolling through my sockpuppets, like a rat picking through bins. She sighs out with each swipe.

'Hun, you've got a ton of cocks. What do they think they're proving?'

'Yeah, I know. Sometimes it's the same guy taking pics from different positions, like he's showcasing it for a competition.'

Fiona smirks. 'Yeah. Imagine these dicks going to a line-up. None of them will stand out'.

I laugh just when a Skype call comes in. It's business time.

'I've got one coming in now', I tell Fiona, hoping that this will remove her scepticism.

'What? Do you know him?'

'He added me a couple of days ago. Added the leopard-skin woman. He's into dressing up. The woman in his pics looks like his girlfriend'. I rattle off the salient facts in descending order of importance.

Fiona is standing unflappable, holding her wineglass at face level while her eyes smile.

'Sooo? Tell me more'.

'It's the anal probe bloke for fuck's sake'.

Fiona's eyes widen along with her speechless mouth. The Skype sound goes off in my laptop. I forgot that I gave this Kevin guy leopard-skin's Skype ID yesterday.

Hey baby. A dialect. Kevin's cheesy one-liner opens the conversation even before I press the webcam down below my face and switch it on. He's wearing a horizontal striped T-shirt that appears to have been shrinking around his beer belly.

I glance at Fiona, opening my eyes wide in a gesture that this isn't a joke. I'm expecting her to roll her eyes and leave. But she grins and folds her arms.

'Is he cute?,' she giggles, before waving a clenched fist in a wanking gesture.

Is someone else there?

I should say 'yes', that it's my best friend being an annoying cow. But I don't want to embarrass him. I signal walking to Fiona. I split my middle and index fingers into two legs and alternate them forward and back in the direction of my door. Her eyes flash and she wags her fingers in a *nuh-uh* gesture.

'No', I lie. 'Just me'.

I've been missing you baby. Let me see your face this time.

'Yeah, Kevin. I've been missing you too'.

Fiona sits on the edge of my bed, just out of range of the webcam panned down on my breasts. It's awkward having this conversation with my friend smirking next to me. But there's nothing I can do about it now.

'I loved it when you crunched your biceps for me. You look so strong'.

Oh yeah? You liked that baby? I can show you more if you like.

The poor man is as happy as someone gatecrashing someone else's party. His buzz is all the more as he never saw this coming. Fiona makes the tiniest sound. It's a giggle suppressed at the back of her throat. My hand nudges my notepad off my desk. I lean down to pick it up at an angle so that Kevin doesn't see my face.

You know I love to play dress-up. I got my alien costume now. My girlfriend hasn't seen it. You can be my first baby.

CATFISH HONEYTRAP

I don't understand him at first. But he actually means it. Fiona is leaning forward now. She extends her finger towards the side of my face in ET fashion. I glance at her and lose it when I see the sad clown expression on her face.

'Wow that's hot Kevin. Show me tomorrow yeah? Got an Amazon delivery now'.

He looks frustrated. Without any warning I lift up my sweater and bra and flash my boobs. I hear a tortured sigh from costume Kevin and hang up. I crack up in giggles.

'Loving that hun. I've got a contender for Aaron'. She laughs as she stands up to leave. I've been so engrossed I can't remember if she's got gym, Aaron or work to go to. I laugh as Fiona says she's going to *phone home*.

Back to business. My Imogen profile on the left-hand computer has just pinged. It's Kerstin's man Chris.

Driving lessons?

Good start. It's a question and not a block. 'Yes, reverse and parallel parking. Pass Plus left me your name in a voicemail.'

Sorry darling. You've confused me with someone else.

This person is not contactable on Messenger

Crap. He's blocked me before I had to chance to reel him back in. Note to self: don't sound too keen or desperate. Let the man's response marinade for a day or two, upload a pretty Imogen pic for him to appreciate in the meantime, then reply.

Luckily Chris accepted Alice's add, too. I'm going to leave his 'hey' DM unread until I've chatted to Kerstin. Each day that passes I'm perfecting the art of being someone else.

The next morning I see what looks like a flyer shoved under my front door. My building's accessed from the outside with a dialpad. So this must be an inside job. I bend down to unfold the A4 page. *Hello downstairs! I'm moving out soon and have a chest of drawers and some bric a brac if you're interested. All free.*

It's the vibrator woman. I'm mildly surprised at her grammatical note. Some of her noises and the fact that the council put her there led me to think she was nuts. Is bric a brac code for a sex toy? I take a second look at the dog-eared note. Its reverse side is a prescription for Citalopram. Hello downstairs indeed. She might have written my name at least. I know she's called Verity because I have the common decency to notice the names on the postboxes on the groundfloor. She might have remembered mine. Holding this handwritten note in my hand feels quaint after all my weeks of online chatting. I suppose the world of vibrators and moving home is still the real one.

Before I leave for work Kerstin leaves me four voicemails explaining her imponderable wayward boyfriend. Chris is crafty. She says crafty in each voicemail. *He's well crafty.* The intonation and hint of estuary Essex 'ah' sound do not bode well. Crafty could cover anything from doubleparking to defrauding pensioners. Then she says his parents are Rotarians, as if that explains the whole thing.

There seems to be no reason why Chris should have rejected Ellie's add, another four, and ignored Linkedin requests and yet succumbed to Alice's allure. Maybe Fiona's IKEA share worked its magic with him. After two exchanges provoked by my pretending I had dropped a call with him (*sorry Chris, I was in the meeting. Sorry for dropping the Skype earlier*) I break through into flirting.

— — — — — — — — — — —

'Sorry my bad. Nice holiday pics btw'.

Yeah, Costa del Sol. Got my tan sorted x'

Chris has five different pics taken from sunloungers. Nothing more is in shot apart from his muscly legs, sandal and the edge of a swimming pool.

'Nice leg by the way.'

Mmhmm

'Where's the other one lol?'

What? Leg?

'Yeah'.

Only got one, sorry babe x

I'm stifling a giggle. It's a good job Harry isn't sitting next to me or he would be asking what's going on.

'Oh, I'm so sorry, what happened?'

The dots appear. They always look ominous. He could still block me like he did with Imogen. I don't know whether to expect a *only joking, none of your business*, or a tragic case of sepsis like Bartholomew.

A shark bit it off when I was rescuing an orphan child from drowning x

I laugh under my breath. I want to go for a piss and get a coffee on my way back but I'm not going to break the flow.

'Oh. You bloody liar! Just saw one of your pics from last week. Have you grown a new leg lol?'

I had 3 to begin with lol

The chat is getting flirtier and he gets a rise from the fact that I'm doing this from my workplace. It's getting easier to switch gears. I make the superhuman transition from deadbeat career nobody to beautiful woman wearing lace underwear finding Chris oh so alluring. Nobody passing by bats an eyelid at my screen. I'm supposed to be focusing on the social media strategy after all. I know how to wipe my search history anyway and I just discovered Incognito mode.

I'm a popular guy, he tells me.

This message sends a shock zinging through me. It's like Chris has just pressed refresh. Then I remember that my five other adds on his profile requested his Facebook friendship. If he's accepted, he might notice all the sockpuppets are friends with my Alice account. I tell Chris I'll brb after getting a coffee. I log out and log straight back into the Imogen sockpuppet and unfriend her from Alice. I log into fat Claire's and scroll down about a dozen DMs and reach Chris. When I click on his question mark response to my lame 'hey stranger' comment I can't find anywhere to click. My heart starts to increase its beat as I figure that Chris has blocked her.

I log out and try the Sandra account. I enter her 'guyshed' password, which I used because her father's pics were exclusively of his spotless garden shed. But the page comes back with a *we didn't recognise this account or password. Set up an account here.*

'Fuck!,' I say. 'Shit!, louder this time.

'Are you OK there?'. It's Aparajita, walking past with a refill for the coffee machine. The whole air comes alive with her perfume.

'Oh, fine. I'm just trying ...'. I type 'guysshed' quickly in case I used a possessive 's' and forgot about it. That doesn't work either.

'It's fine, Aparajita. Just thought I'd lost something but it was backed up'. Note to self: Don't shout out when there's a fake woman on my screen. Delete search history, too.

Aparajita smiles and walks away in an exaggerated semi-circle, putting as much distance as possible between herself and the freak that I am. I just swore at a computer like it's the 1990s. As if I was some IT novice who had just unplugged the modem. But I should not swear at them; I should swear *by* them. I reach down to check my phone. I log into Alice and text Chris *sorry got sidetracked. Chat later?*

*****

After work I dig out my box files to check the passwords. 'Guyshed' was for one of the male profiles. Ian has got a reply from a Lizzie young mother who says she's engaged. I'l check that later. I log into the main laptop and quickly cancel the adds from all my profiles bar Alice. I think I got away with it. Then Fiona comes over to show me some more testimonials she's finished for my Parsnip website. But there's an expectant grin on her face. She's more interested in cosplay man than my emerging sleuth activities.

'Have you sent anyone your own pics?', she asks.

'I have'.

'What? Not *nudes*?'.

'No, for fuck's sake. Not even of my face. Just thighs and my boobs one time'.

'That Sandra bio you showed me. Don't you think this is getting a bit, well, a bit much hun? *Not here for a good time, here for a long time.* It sounds desperate'.

She huffs and presses her arm in a teapot angle to her waist. Her poise is the analogue version of tearing out all my fakes, probably before mouthing off about stalkers, CRB checks and OCD. Then she gives me the look of a self-assured know-it-all.

'Also those leopard-skin pics. It looks cheap. She might as well be twisting a look over her shoulder to show off her tits and arse'.

She seems to have forgotten the whole point of creating characters. Hundrum people stuck in dead-end jobs and relationships, anxious women, frustrated men. But she's still scornful, staring at my screen with one hand on her hip and the other running through her hair.

'Why not her? She looks hot, and that sleek dress is classy'. She puts her glass down and leans over my back. 'There!', she points at the screen.

'You can tell she works in finance'.

'I know what I'm doing Fiona. Besides you're free to check in whenever.

We're linked on the Ipads. Anyway, what about him?'

I show her my first male account. Tall Eminem-lookalike with some bricklaying pics among his selfies. This guy, I explain, looks like an escort.

'Imagine him in a suit instead of workclothes, with a Michael Kors watch, minimalist furniture, and some fuck-you money to be able to refuse upfront payment'.

Her poise is not changing. Her eyes convey disapproval, patronisation.

Then she leans over to scroll down the shaved-headed man's bio.

'Seriously, Faye, look at these messages he got last year. *Glad to see you're out* and *I bet it feels good to be home after all that time.* He's a criminal, not a freaking model'.

She's pissing me off. So what if he was in prison? She looks away and then back at me, as if expecting a punchline. There isn't one. I'm serious.

Fiona seems to have crossed a threshold into incomprehension.

'Faye, look. You've had your fun. What don't you give it a rest for a bit?'

'Rest?'

'Why don't you go back to therapy? You know it's normal to get relapses from time to time'.

I exhale in a huff and keep scrolling. This *is* therapy. I think it's therapy for other people too. Rather than endless scrolling through gossip on celebrities, thinking about people they'll never know, at least with me there is a human being behind the posts and adds. My real self is emerging through these multiple identities. And luckily my real self turns out to be sexy, creative, and interested in making money.

'Seriously, hun, you look miserable now. Jon's moved on. None of this is going to bring him back. An ex should stay an ex. Even if you got Jon back it wouldn't be the same. You'd never be able to trust him again'.

CATFISH HONEYTRAP

What does she think I'm doing here? 'Ex' sounds like a No Trespass sign. But trespassing is what's getting me up in the mornings. Besides, this is becoming bigger than bitchface.

'I'm fine, Fiona. Seriously, I've never felt better.' As I look back at her face the wide-eyed condescending look is there. It's as if she's waiting for me to yield to her suggestion. 'What does DTF mean?.'

'Down to fuck'. Her stare widens at me, as if my ignorance about acronyms has closed the case. 'You never had any social media before the whole Jon drama. It's full of freaks and stalkers and I'm worried it's going to get to you'.

I'm not yielding to her concern. I'm a professional now. I play her a male automated voicenote recording. It backfires. I tried to add background noise from a youtube video to overlay the Stephen Hawking voice. But all I get is a six-second mumble. Fiona gives me an eye-roll.

'For fuck's sake, after all your blogs and Tumblr boasts about your sex life, you're worried I'm overdoing it?'

'Yeah. I keep getting horrible anon messages. I used to reply to them but I just started ignoring them. The haters piss off if you pretend they don't exist. Faye, just let it all slide. Don't get sucked in'.

'I know exactly what I'm doing though'. Poor Fiona doesn't know the whole story.

She rolls her eyes again, and is heading back, she says. She thinks I'm jealous. But she's not cool. She said I lost Jon because I kept trying to pin him down when he didn't want to be pinned down. And whenever I asked for details she deflected to Aaron and her ideal relationship, full of freedom and choice. But the lines around her eyes tell a different story. She's too old, like me, to be cool. She wouldn't have asked me to stalk him with catfish adds if she was cool. And nobody gives a flying fuck about her posts on eyeliner and lipgloss.

She sighs and places her handbag strap on her shoulder. She checks her phone.

'Marathon practice hun. See you later'. She squeezes my shoulder on her way out.

'One more thing Faye'. She turns to face me with my door ajar. 'The ones who want affairs. They're not going to be on social media are they? Their wives and girlfriends will be onto them in no time'.

I smile back at her. She really has no idea, bless her.

*****

I need to go shopping but I don't want to accompany Fiona after our disagreement. It could have been worse. She didn't offer *constructive criticism*. It's admirable of her to put me first, to advise and cajole. But the text she sends me later linking me the Match dating site is as subtle as a loudhailer. She doesn't know just how much she has helped. She got me the website and my icebreaker honeytrap. Her Skype sex with New York boy is the best pretext I can come up with to sustain a sexy chat without needing to reveal myself on a webcam. Fiona's part of this now, complicit in the Facebook rise even without knowing the details.

I take the bus into Croydon. My notifications on my smartphone start pinging with Kerstin's pleas. My blood rises. My smartphone makes my new business real in a way that sitting at home in front of laptop screens does not. Six pings come in quick succession. I can hardly do anything from the bus and Kerstin's boyfriend troubles are not going to change my schedule. I reply with brief 'don't worries' and 'I'll get back to you tomorrow'. There's a class of needy women for whom I'm part therapist, part sleuth.

When I meet up with Fiona later, she's with Jake and a gay guy I remember from last year because he showed me a short story he published about a Satanic gnome. Fiona keeps ordering wine but beer would pace me better. I'm already drunk when we arrive at gay guy's flat later. It's a sleek place filled with Tom Ford cosmetics. There's bare Victorian brick and what he claims is a soundproof window for the sake of his saxophone playing. He's got a new script ready on a Kindle but nobody's in the mood to read it. As Fiona faffs around the kitchen I feel Jake's hand land clumsily on my butt. I don't like men reminding me of my apple figure and this advance has come out of the blue. I freeze but don't say anything. I haven't given him any signals this evening so I feel pissed off. What a shitty way this would be to start a new relationship anyway. His hand can't stay for ever on me. It feels so awkward because it's impossible for me to lean into his advance or to rebuff him without both our mutual honour remaining intact. I feel his heavy breath of moderate intoxication and his hand starts to move to my waist. I'm not going to explain consent to a man who already gets it. I move away and snap his hand down.

'What? Don't you want to?'. He looks at me with that gawky incredulousness from the Brighton pier. 'Sorry, I thought you wanted to'.

'No'. I can't be bothered explaining myself or soothing his ego.

'Are you sure?'

Just because I'm newly single and Fiona sees me as her charity case I'm supposed to like him? Or Fiona thinks I'm desperate enough to take anyone? With some staggered breaths and clammy feeling in my hands, I make my excuses and go to get a cab. Fiona's busy getting something out of a kitchen cupboard and while gay guy's back faces me. There's a faint familiar smell of spices coming from the steel tray holding jars of turmeric coriander and cumin. I don't want to wait to interrupt their chat, only for a half-drunk Fiona to hit me with an *aaaw hun*. I grab coat, bag and phone in the blink of an eye and go straight out. There's no cab in sight so I take the five-minute walk to the tube station. The early summer smell emanating from the walls of the Circle Line reassures me that I am back in solo mode.

Half an hour later I board my bus to my flat, Men and women are busily tapping their phones. Earphones are plugged in. Everyone's face is cast down, focusing on screens. I see Fiona has been texting me. *U ok? WTH did you go? Call me now.* I can't think what got into her.

Jake's not even that close to her. I enter my passcode to reply but get refused. Only then do I realise it's her phone I'm holding and she has texted from mine. I enter her birthday as the 6-digit code and text with apologies. I'll see her tomorrow and we can swap phones then. As my bus heads home I scroll through her phone. Why does she have so many apps? She's got a Marathon-training app, a budget planner, Facebook, Twitter, Linkedin, and enough others to fill the screen. Her tumblr is messed up. She has loads of anonymous messages. Some are nice. They agree with her plea for lemon-grass tea laced with honey and pollen. This is the best hayfever blocker for long-distance runners. Then there are smarmy messages, probably from men, saying *you're amazing! Send this to mutuals and spread the love!* Then she gets nasty ones. *How desperate are you for attention luv?* And *put your tits away you dumb cow.*

There's a layer of voyeurism I can't long entertain with my best friend. Instead I log into her Linkedin. It's curious to see a Marketing profile for real, and the inevitable dozens of high-powered contacts in her feed. There's a green-eyed executive who looks too impressive to be younger than thirty. *Marco Prendergast*. What a weird combination, as if it's a password or an anagram of something. I scroll up and down his list of transatlantic contacts and Ivy League education, clicking likes and a connect before I remember it's not my phone or account. As my stop looms into view I put Prendergast out of mind.

When I get home I down a crisply chilled single Chardonnay and land backwards onto my bed with laptop over my belly. I want to shut down and switch off. Scrolling through my growing Facebook accounts are doing for me that whole bottles of wine and pizzas used to. I advance into my own little world or multiple identities, growing acceptances of my adds, as my new venture grows each day I take several hours away from it. Half my time I spend on networking my sockpuppets. No-one can tell these random accounts from each other beyond the profile pics. No-one stands out. But they ripen with

CATFISH HONEYTRAP

duration, likes and adds. These vacant online identities get added by strangers, linked to advertising.

They're online sirens filtering the real cheaters from the chancers.

*****

I'm weeks into my PI work. I'm used to taking the 62 route up the Old Kent Road. It's longer than the old way but the buildings and landmarks hold no resonance for me, no memories of my time with my ex. I alight behind my office and treat myself to a Pret meatball followed by a double hot chocolate.

As I take my seat a handsome silver fox man about forty is getting kudos stares from some of the women. He's got a toddler daughter who is doing a dance at his feet after repeatedly pressing a three-second blast of music on a toy. The delighted-looking girl obeys her dad's command to sit in an alcove and await her hot chocolate. The Polish waitress adds thick cream to the little girl's drink up to an impossible peak. As the coffee machine growls silver fox takes a call on his smartphone. He lowers his voice saying 'babe' three times. *Can't talk now babe, with family.* He looks like one of Fiona's clients I met last year. The girl's music toy falls to the floor. It's an open goal, like a physical version of the honeytraps I've been setting online. I stand up and walk to the fallen toy. I pick it up and present it to silver fox who has just turned to me holding his drinks. This is my moment.

'Hi. Sorry, your little one dropped this'.

My smile slams the brakes on his jovial face. A stern look bears down on me. I feel suddenly exposed, as if caught in the middle of an illicit transaction. This was going to be my chance. He was supposed to say *oh thanks, she's such a butterfingers*. Then I could have giggled and said something like *hey, aren't you Tom/Tim/Terry or whatever from blah blah?*. Then he could have laughed pityingly. *Sorry darling. I'm so-and-so from wherever.* Then a quick mental note and I would be on his arse on Facebook this evening. Handsome silver fox added by a few of my profiles. He would accept at least one and I would get to stake out his wife with another sockpuppet, whichever girlfriend he was chatting to just now with another, and the blackmail detective work would begin. I wonder how much business I could initiate by treating myself more often to anti-social coffees. But this silver fox does not bite. He's onto me, or is repulsed by my smile. It's back to the catfish trenches for me. I go back to my seat, wrap my fingers around the comforting warmth of my mug, and scroll through my smartphone. All men are potential cheaters, especially if they're handsome like this silver fox. I remember the green-eyed Marco Prendergast man. After scrolling down an implausibly large number of five individuals with that name, I locate him on Facebook and add him.

New month. I should stick a calendar on my wall. One month of catfishing, of creating biographies from nowhere. My therapist told me to stop being methodical with other people. They have their own lives and plans and I need to swim with the chaos. But online I can forget all that and regain my feeling of control. I don't have to replay Jon's non-committal shrugs when I used to ask him questions like what if we couldn't have a baby, what if my OCD turned into schizophrenia like with my grandmother, what if his career went into a tailspin. Here it's not like work either, where I skim emails and answer just one or two of the questions asked in the hope of stalling the customer till hometime. As a PI I'm invested. Besides, after a few days my profiles generate a life of their own. A like on a advert for the latest Ipad, a share of some fashion from one sockpuppet to another, a random message posted on a random profile: all these fake lives and personalities hum away to my satisfaction, bestowing growing plausibility with each day that passes. The world's moved on since the wonders of dial-up Internet and chunky computers of my childhood, when I got bullied for forcing two floppy discs into a Mac computer because it had a sign saying *double density*. So many small parts, moving cogs, interested parties.

CATFISH HONEYTRAP

The men are easy. Plain-faced men with suspicious job titles. More graphic designers than I can shake a stick at. There's one called Mike who's hooked on my bitchface profile. I found a Taiwanese woman living in Shoreditch who's satisfyingly overweight for my parody of Jon's lifestyle lover. Mike's been liking my shitposts of her diet in a working week posts (*What I eat as a busy person, what I eat as a grateful person, what I eat as a vegan*). So far all his messages have been charmingly non-sexual. I don't realise straight away that I was the one who added him after checking the likes on the Bartholomew Garner dedication. Other contacts are off-putting. Weird fish-holders and musclemaxx pics are a turnoff. A hot-looking guy spoils it when I notice his silly hipster cardigan is buttoned up wrong. But the women are more work because of the tons of selfies and my need to biographise them.

Screenblindness teaches me the genius of old-school flashcards. The internet is everything to me, but it multiplies by a thousand the risk of my creative and factual mind overlapping. I alphabetise two drawers of biographical details, one of the growing list of real clients, and the other of the burgeoning catfish details pouring out of my own head. There is a stack of A5 notepaper with square holes in the margin where it has been ripped out for the ringbinder. On each I list the name and bio details. Mike is the practice for creative and factual. He is disarmingly frank and offers slice-of-life details which I template for my imaginary profiles. *Mike Garner. 31, IT consultant. Graduated from Manchester Met, 2:2, but did a Masters. Been in London 7 years. Lives in a house-share. Takes anxiety meds and helps with a charity.* Charity. Bartholomew. All my stalking does not obliterate my sensitivity towards the individual.

The next punter is Cherayar, a PA engaged to another bloody graphic designer. She complains she's trapped in a threesome, her, Bradley, and Bradley's smartphone. Then she checked his phone one time when he darted out fast enough for it not to require a password entry. She saw him chatting to loads of girls. It always starts with a 'poke'. I can't work out if that's a pun or the Facebook gimmick whose place in the chat hierarchy I still can't make out. I tell her there's still time to nip this in the bud. Bradley accepts my catfish add the next day. He is mathematically handsome, dressed in a Scandinavian crime drama jumper, a restrained stubble and a bad-boy stud in his right ear. He accepts my new I-wen Tai add like a man slumming it with someone plainer than him. The dowdier the better. It reeks of authenticity.

The hardest part is keeping track of all the stories I'm making up. It's like a human form of Sudoku. After my first ten catches I notice that my chat turns into the same, insipid flirting mixed with tidbits of biographical detail. My interest lapses in my real Facebook account. When an old uni friend called Summer messages me from Costa Rica and rattles on about her boyfriend proposing to her on board a yacht I pacify her with a heart and a virtual hug GIF.

Got a big wedding to plan lol

Another heart from me. Then it's back to business. Summer deserves a cursory reply. She spent a month sleeping homeless on my sofa back at uni and kept leaving used coffee granules clogging up my machine. I never got any real thanks. Now she gets the Latin American engagement tour and some Andrew in tow.

If I stick with this I-wen Tai woman, then I have to create other friends and relatives. I need to set up a couple more sockpuppet accounts. I need some shitposts in I-wen's profile. A few puke emojis at her food posts, and a random DM to one of her catfish complaining about I-wen silencing her, then she becomes as fully rounded in her friendships as her butt in those jeans she was showing off at some weird dance party. I should set up a Qiang Yu account for bitchface's mystery lover. But the stakes are high and there's a chance Jon might already have sensed something from that man from Match already. I don't want a fakelooking Facebook account to reveal that mystery man. I'm still hoping to fuck them with him.

CATFISH HONEYTRAP

I have to know something about East Asian names, even if Xiao and Xiu, Liao and Liu, might as well be the same for me. Am I supposed to scroll through pages on Wikipedia working out the history of Hong Kong or Taiwan, or wherever? I lose trust in keeping tabs on the hundreds of saved files. I trust my handwriting and the copious space of my A-Level English binder ominously labelled in black marker-pen 99-00.

There's enough space in each folder to fit hundreds of pages. Or double if I store each entry as A5 paper tagged on a single clasp. A thought dawns on me. I log back into my own Facebook account and go to Summer's message. Her chat is still Active. She must be eight hours or so behind GMT.

'Hey Summer! Sorry I was really busy just now. That's fantastic news!

Wow, a wedding to plan!'

My message is seen right away. Then her dots appear. She's probably lazing in a beachside hammock with a smartphone and Andrew bringing her juice.

Yeah I'm thinking of that Herstmonceux castle place in Sussex. How are you anyway Faye x?

'Oh, great thx. Doing more stuff in my job. Wow, Herstmonceux. Just googling it now. It looks really big'. I scroll up and down Summer's Facebook pics. There's a bikini one from yesterday where she's staring directly into the lens with her lip curled. She's got her pinched face and slim body. But each selfie is with a frown, as if she's got an annoying relative taking each pic.

Yeah I'm going to invite at least a hundred and Andrew's got loads, too.

They've got an opening in November.

'Oh cool. Five months isn't a ton of time to get the invites out.' I'm clicking on her Friends now. There are hundreds. This is looking good.

Yeah. They've got a zillion different wedding options and I can't decide lol. I just want to fix the date now and worry about the rest later x

'Haha yeah. Don't need to worry about that when you're sipping cocktails on a yacht.'

Lol Andrew rented it for a day. Back at the hotel now. But we've got another 2 wks here and Cancun

'Yeah, makes sense. Listen Summer. Let me help. What you need are some 'Save the Date' invites sent out.' I'm remembering my friendship with her was only skin-deep, one where we hung out lots without really connecting. Maybe that's good for what I'm proposing next.

Yeah. I was thinking that. I would just email everyone but that looks crap.

'Lol yeah. Why don't you email me the names and addresses of the people you're going to invite? They're all in the UK right?'

Wow, yeah. Well Andrew's inviting some of his old colleagues from Frankfurt, but yeah. Would you really send them out for me Faye?

'Course Summer. I want to help where I can. Been ages since we caught up, so it's the least I can do. Anyway, I'm working for the council. I can print out the addresses on envelopes for free.'

Oh wow, you're a sweetheart Faye! If that's really free to print out the addresses, that's so cool. But don't let me get you into trouble x I'll send you the money for the stamps and the invite cards once I've settled on a design.

'No worries at all Summer. Send me the names and enjoy the rest of the holiday x'

You're a sweetheart Faye. Send my best to Jon. Hasta luego! xx

*****

I have purpose. I no longer have the Sunday evening feeling of dread of the week ahead. I have not touched wine in four days. I'm now an enthusiastic tea drinker, getting through five or six hot brews per day, relishing the taste of what in the Chardonnay days used to taste like tepid swill clogged with a bag at the bottom. The colour comes back to my cheeks. I am a natural brunette with alluring dark eyebrows. Now I look powerful, sphinx-like, poker-faced, the perfect persona behind the multiple identities. I scoff at bitchface's posts. Her false eyelashes make her little skull look ridiculous.

Besides, Summer has supplied me with the details of 116 people. About 90 are in couples. More than the average have loaded-sounded double barrels and trust fund giveaway names like Victor, Dominic and JJ. There's even a Hortensia I remember from uni who claimed her dad invented the ATM or something. Those I can't find on Facebook are on Linkedin. Fifty new men of cheatable age are added, DM'd or pended. It's the biggest investment of a single evening. I go to bed buzzing with ambition but I also know I need to unwind.

I'm just about to put my phone under Jon's pillow but check on Marco Prendergast just in case. He's replied and is online.

What's your jam?

Jam. Nice gambit. One for the memory bank.

'Strawberry.'

My reply is seen.

Outstanding. What you up to x?

'I'm up to nunnya'.

Nunnya?

'Yep. Nunnya Business'.

I log out with a smirk and log into Ian. Lizzie's *hi what's up?* needs an answer.

'Good, you?'

The dots appear right away. She's up late for someone with a toddler.

Do I know u sorry?

What am I supposed to say? *No, you don't know me but I'm a fully-grown woman pretending to be Ian and messaging you because you look like you're in a dysfunctional relationship and either you or your fiancé are going to stray.*

'You appeared on my suggested friends list and I thought you were really attractive x'.

Oh.

Seen. Silence. What would a man say in this situation? What would Marco say?

'What's your jam?'

*****

Sometimes online stalking pays you back without any effort. The next day my check on Rightmove confirms it. Hoi's flat is sold. Moving in together with Jon after two months seems desperate. But the sinking feeling in my gut stops me feeling any pity for my ex, not after he resisted moving in with me for years. I press my cheek into my palm and search her address on Google Street view.

When I get home to start my real job I keep thinking about my dildobombing and where the happy couple are moving to. I try to focus on catfishing but the doubt about my intrusion is distracting me. I'm logged in as fat Claire and she's hooked a middle-aged Cypriot property developer who has a silence rule. No speaking is allowed. Not even one word asking to repeat his question from his muffly portakabin. He gestures with his animated forefinger, waving it upwards in a command to remove my blouse. The revelation of my breasts elicits a grinning nod. Then he raises both in an open-palmed gesture, his fingers moving upwards. I correctly take this as a command to stand. I stick my arse out. I'm wearing John Lewis knickershorts stretched over my bulge in a faithful imitation of Claire. I sit and see him grinning wider. There's a knocking sound reverberating on Skype. He stops and seems to glance upwards, as if there's a door in front of him with a window that someone from outside can peer through. He looks back down at me and the grin returns. There's more knocking, louder this time.

'Do you want us to stop?', I ask. I've just broken the silence rule.

'Yes', he replies, heavy under his breath. Then he zips himself back up and stretches across his desk, as if going to activate an intercom.

'Sorry,' I reply, as if it's my fault he has the hang-up on silence and my fault his colleague is interrupting.

Without looking at me ends the call, then blocks me.

I breathe out with a murmur, half-laughing, half-crying. Maybe having that creep treat me like shit is karma for my antics at Hoi's home. I prop my elbow on the table and press my forehead into the palm of my hand.

Maybe Fiona is right. I haven't seen my therapist in weeks.

It's almost a quarter to ten and I realise that I've eaten nothing but a cereal bar all day. Way to go for dieting. I've got time to dart to the Costcutter and buy some bread, cheese and fruit. I'm the only one in the shop. The woman behind the counter looks offended when I enter at 9:55. I get home, eat bread and cheese, and listen to the dulcet tones of Kevin McCloud on *More4+2*.

Chapter 5

Most women care about underwear. But I can honestly say that with the possible exceptions of pornstars and dominatrices, nobody spends more time thinking about underwear than a catfish stalker. It's not just me choosing colours, tights, panties and thongs for my own taste. It's my business to pander to the client. When you have a roster running into double figures, it won't do to remember that this one gets turned on by red frilly knickers and the other by popping out tits in a bra. You need every likely variation of underwear ready to respond to the punter's demands and prevent his bloodless brain from asking for a face pic.

People are weird. All those big-tit bimbos with their stupid boobjobs, that botox victim that looked weirdly like the Easyjet woman who had made me stow a bag that was half a kilo overweight, even that genuinely classy PA woman with the curly red hair. They all got sussed. No biters. The men pass or leave the pics with a like. One man who looks like a cheatable walk-on for *The Only Way is Essex* busted my small talk in one minute. ('hey, are you the same Alistair I'm working with? x'. *Wtf.* 'Sorry I'm working with three different Alistairs so thought I'd check x'. *I don't care if you know a hundred. I know tons of people with your name are you a retard or somet.*) Then some of their girlfriends shitpost me in their DMs. My bimbo boobs are fake, or should be put away because I'm a stupid bitch. My teeth are stupid. The worst comments come from women in their forties. *In case u didn't get it last time Mitchell is my husband so don't love heart his pictures mate.* It's as if school bullying has skipped twenty years. But I'm having the last laugh this time.

Maybe my ex is an even bigger prick than I give him credit for. I'm two glasses into scouring up and down bitchface's street on Google. I'm not apologetic but I'm also not completely comfortable with what

CATFISH HONEYTRAP

I've been doing. But the rewards are flowing in and who is really being harmed anyway?

I go back to the frumpy foreign sockpuppet. She could be a fat loser version of bitchface, but from Taiwan instead of Hong Kong. I google common Chinese names and surnames, set up I-wen Chang, just changing her surname. I add an unflattering profile pic of her in glasses, and a post showing her chubby butt on a Tube escalator. I add my own likes, knowing that nobody's likely to hover over this token overweight friend of a dozen Carlas, Charlottes and Helenas. I don't even return to I-wen Chang until the end of the week, and almost forget to get the catfish biography (the real person called Jos is a Taiwanese social worker, or Masters student, unclear which, since most of her Linkedin is in Chinese). But I'm relieved I do. I've got 21 DMs in the space of a week. To think that some of the best-looking men with the nicest-looking girlfriends are stooping to this. Maybe plain is the new thrill for these guys. Maybe social workers are hot. Or maybe just because she's foreign.

I give her a backstory. I keep her chubby and boring, dependable, and everygirl, Nescafe not Espresso. Her brave bikini was supposed to be an inspiration for women above dress size 16. I post a link of a *Vogue* model wearing a hipster dress, adding a plea *how much weight do I need to lose to wear this?* But the next day some women have piled on with sympathy. *That model's waist is unreal. So shit. Don't they eat?* God bless online ads for enraging other women who know they'll never look like the girl on the screen. But it's attracting as many likes from men. I definitely need to prioritise her bio. Maybe frumpy girl got stranded in London after the Icelandic volcano erupted and decided to stay on and make the best of it, spending another year in England. Too convenient. I dig deep into her Facebook posts and see a link to something called Weibo. I imagine her life, an early riser, for my convenience, a failed student of pilates. Maybe she has a demanding life with underprivileged kids, mentally and emotionally exhausting, so she never gets to exercise her fat butt properly.

I place her somewhere unfashionable in south-east London. I walk down Walworth Road. I enter an oriental minisupermarket on my way, and stalk the aisles in the hope of inspiration. As I walk back out onto the street, the sight of a woman looking like an international student taking a camera call showing a box of mochi triggers an idea in my head. I take a three-second vid outside the Cantonese minisupermarket in Camberwell, keeping a sideways shot to avoid my own Caucasian reflection in the front window. I enter to take random pics of frozen dumplings and loads of Korean stuff that's all over this Chinese shop for some reason. I post half the pics when I get home and become the kimchi queen. I save the vid for authentic 'sorry can't chat now, just out shopping' moments. I-Wen has lived with me all week. I'm starting to forget where she ends and I begin. My therapist once said something of the dangers of cross-addiction. If I suddenly stop drinking, then taking hard drugs would compensate. But he never mentioned the option of crossing into two dozen made-up personalities. Unless I missed that part when he opened a bag of crisps and took one at a time after speaking, then chewing without crunching as I replied.

The next day I-wen's become a Facebook hit. Her mochi pics have got a dozen likes, most of them from people I don't recognise, and a couple of indecipherable comments in Chinese. I try learning a smattering of Cantonese. Then Wikipedia tells me that Taiwan is Mandarin. That looks even harder. There's a Mandarin class meeting on Saturday mornings in a college sports hall. I go once and it seems a set-up. I'm the only non-Asian person there, and everyone else is a Hong Konger seeming to want nothing more than perfect calligraphy. I try but I'm hopeless. I can't distinguish the different characters and the logic escapes me. A mouth for 'ask' looks like a Christmas present to me. I give up. I won't go again. I reinvent I-wen as born in Taiwan but grown up in the USA. That would explain the robotic voice generator

CATFISH HONEYTRAP

I'm starting to use. It works better if I add background restaurant or bar noises, then it's foolproof. The mufflier the better. Nobody wants a female Stephen Hawking voice.

I am seeing what people do and don't want. Pretty women do not answer DMs. Slim women usually don't answer DMs. Average women might. Fat women, ugly women, certainly will if I'm sending the add from the Eminem-lookalike. Men are similar. The fat, the plain, the unhappily married, will dabble at least. Handsome men are harder to lure. Like pretty women they sense fakeness in an infuriating absence of cosmic justice. Leopard-skin bimbos and pouty-lipped stunners get blocked or ignored. My best chance with them is my faithful I-wen. The plain, good-natured, chubby Chinese woman is having the virtual time of her life.

I finish the Chardonnay in one sitting tonight. I scroll through I-wen's contacts. I need to create a smattering of pretty friends as a gateway drug. One of them looks amazing. She must be an aunt or teacher. She's in her fifties but doesn't look a day over 30. Stereotypes about Asian women ageing well are true. I'm so glad I can control my flirting. I only zoom on my body beneath my face. The exotic voice generators spare the cringe of cosplaying another culture and of wishing the ground would swallow me up.

I check her messages a final time before calling it a night. Damon from Summer's wedding list has replied to my 'Sorry for my add but are you the Damon doing the social work research at London Metropolitan?'.

Sorry, I-wen, that's not me. I'm in Torquay, about 20 miles from Exeter. Don't know anything about London Metropolitan sorry x

Two hours later he sent a second message. *You live in London then? You look Chinese.*

I reply 'Sorry my bad. I located the other Damon now x'

It's seen right away. A married man pushing forty is messaging me at midnight. His wife is probably sleeping next to him.

Haha ok love. Your loss. You just missed out on the best-looking Damon in the UK x

'Oh, just saw your profile pic now,' I lie. 'Yeah you don't look like the typical social worker lol'.

I log out of I-wen. Damon is keen so I need to slowburn him for a few days. If we're still messaging at the end of the week, I'll send a Parsnip share to his wife's Facebook page.

Before bed I scroll down Marco's posts. Yesterday he called me a pervert for liking his gym pic. I replied with an angel emoji and he countered with a devil. He's taken the gymrat stereotype and run with it. Now I'm scrolling through his own East Asian fad. His obsession with Japanese karate makes him as pretentious as me. There's something about being invited to a So-Kyokushin karate, and how he *gets in purple to symbolize power.*

'You OK there dickhead? Missing me?'

Marco replies with an emoji wink, then a *sorry babe, I'm just going to do some meditating. Chat later x.*

Of course he fucking is. Anyone else volunteering this information would sound like a grinning David Blaine, vibing platitudes of mindfulness. The buzz of an attractive chat partner is the icing on the cake for my new magic of creation. I feel like a musician or a writer. I bet a great novelist would rather die than stop writing. But unlike Duffy or Stephen King I have no competition, no agent, no publicity. It's just little old unassuming me stuck in my bedsit messing with people's lives.

I check on Marco. He's written *missing me already? x* and has sent a foursecond voicenote of his shower.

I give his karate invitation a like and stalk his friends list. There's a Russian-looking Anastasia based in London with an English surname and a penchant for monobrow selfies. I add her. She looks like a supermodel and might welcome frumpy I-wen lurking in her contacts.

I slide my phone under my pillow and go to sleep.

CATFISH HONEYTRAP

*****

Fiona's new shoes are so big that they've become the main thing about her. And here is little old me in my tiny slip-ons, putting a new dent in the universe of online relationships while she strolls boss-like around my bedsit with her hair flopped back like a youthful afterthought. As she follows me to my laptops I sense a resentful stride behind me, cold feet rather than shyness. She was so supportive to begin with. Now she doesn't want to know. I'm outsmarting her tumblr-ass brain and she doesn't appreciate it.

As Fiona sits on my bed and obligingly shares likes and shares stuff with my accounts, I finish creating a couple more sockpuppets. I find a sleek businesswoman, with the sort of red hair complexion that made her look either 25 or 45. Her black sealskin suit is good for a profile pic.

I file away a dozen other pics to trickle uploads over the days.

I remember Fiona's advice. I need to 'pivot' and be 'pro-active', to make up detective work where none is needed. I need business advice. I watch *The Apprentice* and all I notice is the importance of 'cash flow'. It's an excuse to get screwed over, or not to try anything in the first place. But I never feel tired or stressed, in contrast to the monotony and concentration of my workplace.

She used to enjoy this, but now she's huffing through each portrait I blow up on my laptop screen. She hovers over the good-looking retro and semi-erotic pics. But the girls all look about twenty, with their heads full of shit. I move onto the normal women, while Fiona stands next to me like a mentor. Then I see her glance towards a Dominoes pizza box next to my laptops, a Mighty Meaty thought bubble all but visible over her lemon-grass dieting head. Her gaze flits back to my screens and her nose flinches like the snob she is.

'You're not in a good mood. Haven't you just done your call with Aaron?'

'Mmmhmm.'

'Well, isn't that supposed to make you feel all flushed and happy?' Fiona eyerolls.

'What is it?.' I just come out with it. I can't handle her sudden switch from hot to cold.

'Are you absolutely positive Aaron hasn't answered any of your fake profiles?'

Odd question to ask. Why would I be hiding anything?

'Yes. Absolutely positive. What is it Fiona?'

She tuts away my question like an impertinence. Then she sits on the edge of my bed, as if wanting to verify.

'Come and check for Christ's sake. It's Alice, Imogen and fat Claire'.

She leans forward, placing her elbow on my desk and cupping the side of her face into her palm. There are so many contacts in each account that I have to use the search bar to get Aaron on the screen. She checks each one in turn. The 'Delivered' sign following each gambit must look suddenly ominous to her. It's as if any normal innocent man would at least read a random DM.

'OK', she says, and breathes out. 'I've decided I need to trust him more'.

'He seems like a good'un for real. Why don't you go out there if you're really thinking he's slipping away?.'

'Yeah, Faye could you delete those accounts? I'm feeling icky about the whole thing now.'

I stifle a scoff on my throat. It's involuntary. I could pretend not to have heard that request. If we were in a noisy bar in Brighton I could have batted it away with a non-committal *yeah sure* before changing the subject. But there's no chance in my deathly silent bedsit. Maybe she meant it as a deflection from my advice about going to New York. She implies her job is so global she could relocate anywhere. But I bet her company wouldn't send her.

'Delete? What do you mean?'

'Yeah just remove them. If you block him he still might log in and see them another way. I don't want to give him any ammunition to start rooting around.'

My heart sinks. Real-world friendship with a woman who has helped me has encroached on my alternative world. I don't like feeling emotionally blackmailed when I'm the only blackmailer here.

'Fiona, these are my best accounts. I can't just ditch them. You just saw all the messages you had to scroll down.'

'Fuck's sake Faye, it's only these three. I'm not asking for much.'

My rage is boiling making me almost dizzy. Fiona set me up with the idea, the Parsnip website, advice, with everything. But why can't she just let me be?

'It's only those three accounts, right? You're not trying to protect me from bad news, are you Faye?'

'Look, I'm logging into all three accounts ok? I'm blocking Aaron on each one. I can't delete the accounts though because they're making me money.'

Fiona stands up in a huff. She pulls her handbag strap over her shoulder and seems to brush imaginary dust off her abdomen.

'Faye, honestly, do you think this makes you happy any of the time? Do you think it makes *me* happy? You don't because you never ask me. This has been on my plate for two months and God knows how much it's been taking up of yours. You're treating me like I'm some fucking ladyin-waiting organising a thousand fucking fake relationships!'

Fiona stutters her breaths twice. She looks on the verge of tears. She shakes back her hair and winds it around itself to make a loose knot at the back of her head. Deep down I do feel ashamed. But I never really asked her to come so far with me. Or at least I don't remember doing it. Besides, I like keeping all the secrets to myself. I'm getting good at it.

'I need to get going. I'll call later if Hoi accepts my add, OK. It's getting dark and I saw some dodgy geezers down in the estate just now.' She stands up and knocks the side of my desk with her hip.

The estate she calls it every time, as if she doesn't live a hundred yards away over the footbridge, and the Adidas ASBOs and teenage mums never make it to her side. Maybe those gentrifying water-fountains they erected shoot out sideways the moment anyone in a tracksuit approaches.

'Listen, Fiona. You've helped me loads. You've helped me more than anyone has. Aaron's blocked now and I won't approach him any more unless you ask me to'. I break my hand free and rub my screen-jaded eye with the palm of my hand. I feel blood flushing back to my cheeks. 'I need to help myself now. I can keep going with this. I don't want to burden you any more. I treasure our friendship over everything else'.

I watch my ultimatum land on her face, immediately changing it from condescending to crestfallen. I feel like I've let her down. I breached the lightness of our relationship, where she would snap me out of my OCD and I would help her put order to her chaos. Now my screenlives have taken over.

'Catch you later hun'.

My heart sinks as soon as she leaves. However right she is my whole body aches to ignore her. For the first time ever I'm winning at something part of me wants to screech out. But I won't be subjected to adult analysis. My mindset like the dozens of personae online is neither young nor old, nor middle-aged. I refuse to be nuanced and reasoned. I know what I'm doing is shallow and immature but shouldn't I be shallow and immature? Six years wasted with Jon has jolted me back to the start, not wisened me with age and introspection.

Cosplay Kevin's girlfriend is asking to Skype me. I accept the video call without a second thought. She looks different this time. Not the angelic pyjama woman with her hair wrapped in a towel like the first time she called me. This time she is dressed formally, as if psyched up to hear the worst. She appears frantic when she finally takes her seat, flapping her dress out like a judge taking his bench. I sigh. Fiona's words are sinking in. I can't bring myself to do it this time.

'I have nothing, I'm afraid. Two different women in my team kept calling Kevin but he made it clear he has a girlfriend and he's not interested in anyone else.'

'Oh'. Her eyes return the angelic look I remember from the first time.

'Really'.

'You've got a good one there Isobel. It's case closed. No payment required'.

'What, really? Are you sure?'.

I feel a warm glow return to my heart. In a way I really don't have anything. I never pretended to try to meet him, and scrolling up and down his latest messages shows he's deleted about half of them. It reads like a redacted MI6 thread. But it's really deleted promises of what he would make me wear and where he would stick his probe.

'Really Isobel. But do me a favour. Add a testimonial to the Parsnip site.'

She's still in love with him, weirdo though he is. Even if he cheated for real he is the sort of man who would see sense and beg for forgiveness, probably with the aid of an engagement ring. I go to my kitchen and run the tap. I watch the water gurgle for ages before it occurs to me to get a glass. I drink a gulp and then remove cutlery from the sink, just so I have something to do with my hands. Fiona assumes I should be feeling degraded and humiliated. But far from it. I've never felt so secure.

Now it's time for real housekeeping. I open Excel on Jon's laptop that always takes forever to load for some reason. I enter 'fee waived' on the Isobel line on the spreadsheet. Then it's back to the fun stuff. I need to add real friends to beef up the profiles. I am in my rhythm of disassociation. I go back to the Joanne Thompson account and take a close-up pic of my eye as a profile pic. I sit Zen-like between amidst my screens like a slender Buddha. I know that having no women on the female profiles is a red flag. It's like a shit house party full of gamers or rugby lads. Too many women would be shit in a party, or a speed-dating event where the men sheepishly don't show. But on Facebook the more women friends the better. I can't let my sockpuppets look like whores. Men like a challenge. They don't want to feel threatened by other men, even when they post weird pics of motorbikes and suffocating fish in their profiles.

*****

Fiona cancels our lunch the next day. Too busy. I leverage it to secure one final favour from her with my Bradley case. We're meeting up on Friday to watch a re-run of *Eat Pray Love* at the cinema after I honeytrap Cherayar's wayward graphic designer. She picked the film in return for agreeing to be a back headshot for my Ellie catfish who's been sexting Bradley for weeks. Before I head out and give a final check on the Parsnip inbox. There's a new message with the subject 'FPIUK Invitation'. It evokes the sense of being spam email from some high street brand, maybe wanting me to answer an online survey for the impossible chance of winning a cash prize. I almost delete the email. At this point the ratio of spam to client a re-runmessages is averaging about three-to-one. But something in the reserved subject header intrigues me. I open the message.

Dear Jacqueline (if I may),

My name is Brian Marsh and I am the forthcoming chair of the Federation of Private Investigators (UK). I hope you don't mind my reaching out to introduce myself on behalf of our organisation. The FPIUK has more than forty years' experience representing the interests of private investigators throughout the UK. We are always on the lookout for new colleagues working in the field. Your name has been mentioned in our last meeting as a newcomer showing particular talent using social media as an investigative tool.

CATFISH HONEYTRAP

With this in mind we would be delighted to invite you to our next annual meeting timetabled provisionally for the autumn this year. We are meeting for a whole afternoon at Hazelworth Castle near Leeds. As an invited guest we would waive the usual attendance fee of £75. We would also invite you (plus a guest) to our buffet lunch, also free of charge.

Please let me know if this sounds of interest. We are on the lookout for fresh blood in our field and would be delighted to meet you in person.

Fiona thinks I should be feeling like a beaten dog. But I feel great. This Brian has given me external validation. Real validation, not the *you're hot* kinds from random clients. I get to the cinema early to make sure Fiona gets here on time and I can see Bradley arrive to wait at the coffee section as agreed. There's a bent postbox listing at a twenty-degree angle, as if a truck reversed into it. I take a quick pic for a lol feed for Iwen. Then there's a sudden commotion and chatter of voices. A boyband celebrity is walking past with his girlfriend and getting bothered by some paparazzi. There's one tall pursuer with an athletic posture in down-at-the-heel attire, a green tracksuit and trainers that look caked in mud for some reason. Either they've been filming something pastoral or the pursuer has just wasted some workman's day by walking through wet cement.

I'm sorry, there's no photographing here, the minder says.

The boyband smiles back fleetingly. But the photographer does not alter his pursuit. He only cocks his abdomen posture back for a moment, as if waiting for a punchline.

It's just our policy, no photographs. It's the same for everyone, I'm afraid.

The minder sounds surprisingly mild-mannered. The tracksuit man is not appeased. He points his camera unabated. It prods in front of the celebrity's face like a weapon. *Just a quick one and I'll be off.*

We said no!. The minder knocks the camera hand out of the way just before a flash ignites fruitlessly. The paparazzo almost loses his grip before the celebrities speed towards a waiting car. He then runs off with perfect symmetry. The next man I see is Bradley. He's wearing smart casual clothes, indicating he's come direct from his graphic design office. I'm willing Fiona to take a fashionable five minutes extra in order to pitch the tension.

When Fiona appears she freezes on the the side of the road and checks her phone, unaware of my presence. She raises her elbow and vanishes her hand behind the back of her head. Then she paces back and forth, looking like she's inventing another reason to stand me up. A couple of joggers go round her without turning their heads. Then she puts her phone back into her handbag and sees me as she crosses the road..

'All good?', I ask, gently flinging pity at her.

'Never been better.'

'Bradley's at the counter.'

Fiona smiles with a hint of weariness at her tiresome OCD friend. But her muscle memory of confidence carries her inside and next to the 6fttall cheat with the posh girlfriend. My phone is ready. I take a vid of the back of Fiona walking to the counter, making sure to film her back from the waist up since my best friend is taller than Ellie. Then two pics of Fiona talking something random to Bradley. I see him prop up the counter in profile, his gaze sweeping over my friend from head to foot. I catch a smile on his face. Another vid, again from the waist up and without showing her face, and we're done.

'What did you say to him?'

'Just, sorry, thought you were someone else', Fiona replies. 'Let's get inside before he tries pulling me hun.'

Poor Bradley can stay stood up in the Parsnip tradition. And Fiona is safe from his attention. He's a straight bloke pushing thirty. There's zero chance he's going to buy a ticket to watch a Julia Robertson film.

As I sit in front of the film I glance at Fiona to my right. She sits granitelike, suddenly old in her silence. Like the celebrity incident outside earlier she seems to be the end of a generation. I am the new. I master the virtual world and leave the Polaroid paparazzi in the dustbin of history. After the film Fiona takes longer in the toilet than usual. I suspect there's another Aaron crisis. I could go inside and ask her but there's too much temptation in the foyer. There's a crowd waiting around for refreshments for one of the next screenings. Two latetwenties-looking men are standing with print-out tickets on the counter.

'*I'm just with Jonny babe. For fuck's sake*'.

I step closer towards him. My relationship crisis radar is fully alert. Girlfriend suspects boyfriend. He ends his call and smirks at the other man.

'*Got you by the balls mate*', he says.

Print-out tickets mean names. Fiona could come back at any moment but I'm going to take my chances. I loosen my handbag strap down my shoulder as I walk towards them and pretend to take a phonecall. I say *hey, sorry what is it?* to my imaginary caller and drop my bag onto the floor next to the counter. Then I say *sorry give me a sec* before slapping our used *Eat Pray Love* tickets next to the men's and pick up my handbag. I stand up and swipe the men's tickets accidentally on purpose before going back to my imaginary friend. *Oh yeah? OK that sounds good to me. I'll check and call you tomorrow.*

'Sorry darling, you took our tickets'. His voice is loud, like a recrimination.

'Sorry, what?'

'Yeah, you put these two on the counter when you dropped your bag'. His eyes flick uncertainly from my face to another woman passing by behind me. His friend adjusts his baseball cap and turns to face me with a smile. It hits me then that he has a birthmark stretching down his left cheek.

'Oh, sorry let me see'. I step towards him, hoping that he'll lower his voice if I'm closer and won't show me up if Fiona sees me like this. I don't need an eyeroll from her followed by a look saying *for fuck's sake, do you never stop!?* I scan the tickets as fast as I can. My eyes are drawn to *INCEPTION* before I spot Hallewell, M and Rossi, J. Two memorable surnames.

'Oh, yeah. Here you are, sorry. Sci-fi's not my thing anyway.' Hallewell or Rossi smiles graciously without an eyeroll.

Fiona is out of the loo and I finally get some uninterrupted chat time with my best friend.

'What do you think of this?'. I show Fiona the email I got from Brian at the FPIUK.

'What's that hun? Dense text. Can't be arsed reading. What's it about?'.

'There a federation of private investigators and they're inviting me to a meeting at a stately home near Leeds'. I hand her my phone and she starts scrolling obligingly.

'*Leeds* Leeds, not Leeds Castle hun?'. Fiona is deftly clicking on the link in the email and checking out the federation's webpage. I'm miffed that Leeds is what she gets out of my big reveal instead of my accolade from the FPIUK, an organisation which I never knew existed until five hours ago.

'Yep. Oop north. I've got a plus one. Wanna come with?'

She frowns at my suggestion. But it looks more in amusement rather than condescension.

'Mmm dunno hun. They're all men. Old farts in cheap suits. Look at the pics. You're best off getting a bloke to go with you.'

'Haha yeah I'll find someone'.

'Jake's got a car'.

'Mm maybe'. Whoever my plus one will be is not going to be Jake. 'A lift would be nice. It's out in the sticks.'

When I get home I check my Facebook and scroll down four Hallewells until I find him. Mark Hallewell from Bromley is using a gorilla as a profile pic but my click reveals more photos of him, including two with his girlfriend. He looks exactly as in the cinema earlier: clean shaved, short brown hair and glasses. The girlfriend called Abbie hugging him is tall and sad-looking. Something about her draws me in as she looks more into Mark than he is into her. I file away Abbie's details. She's slim so I log into two fat-girl accounts and scroll down her posts. I like one of her jokes and two fashion pics, to make her look good. If Mark takes off I'll get ready to add her. Then I log into two more accounts, get one to add Mark and get the other to like a couple of his posts. I file away his details in the pending tray, making a note of *likes Inception film*. Then I log into two sockpuppets to add three different friends from his contact list. I try the same with J Rossi but the cinema man doesn't seem to be any of them.

I reply to Brian's email showing interest and wanting to know more about his organisation. I'm done for this evening. I log into my real Facebook account and check on Fiona's updates. I look so fat next to her. Was I always only her token fat friend? There to make her look good? Maybe all we have in common now is our shared past. If I met her now out of the blue aged 28 I'm sure we would not be friends.

My whole bedsit is a mess. I haven't cleaned in a week and there's enough dirty washing dumped across my floor to allow someone to walk barefoot without touching the carpet underneath. My desk is bulging with piles of notes detailing plots and biographical information ranging from Cosplay Kevin to the Russian trophy wife Anastasia whose husband is offering me a grand just to see if she's cheating on an eastern European man on a building site in Lewisham. The money's rolling in but I seem to be living like a student. I need to discipline myself.

I'll skip lunch. Losing some weight will get one up on Fiona. She has an appalling diet and I expend at least as much energy as her. Only genetic injustice condemns me to an apple-shaped frump. I have a couple of friends from back home who I see precisely three times a year, for birthday catch-ups. They don't invest the time beyond these drinks. But they don't patronise like Fiona either. I resist the Sara Lee in the fridge. I should try one of Fiona's self-cleansings, when she consumes nothing but lemon-grass tea for two days and then binges on a Mighty Meat Domino's pizza. Slimming will make me a better model if I ever need to Skype catfish as an attractive woman. But pizza is impossible to get right when you live alone, and I'm crap at flirting anyway. My erotic chat is like a straight-to-video film. I can't think of anything exciting.

I'm just channelling Fiona's freaky New York boyfriend bollocks all over again. Luckily, men are idiots. My latest catch says 'sexy lady,' then 'laaaydy' with a drawn-out guttural tone. He fucking says it again, then gives a laugh, the worst laugh I've heard, all insincere, sad and pathetic. He deserves to be called Wayne. He switches on his webcam even though mine remains off. He is frowning, seeming genuinely confused by the absence of a pouty-lipped face on his screen. He stumbles over some anatomical puns on my assumed name. I tell him my boyfriend is watching my face from his office in New York and doesn't know that I'm secretly watching Wayne. He pulls down his jeans and triumphantly flops arse-first into the sofa. He's got a semi propping up his boxers even before his hand finds his crotch. He's never seen my face so I'm safe to use my own voice. I give him a couple of voicenotes, telling him I have to mute my boyfriend each time. My focus is only on Wayne. *That's good, my laaaady. Keep focusing on me.*

It's easy to be quick and sassy with this cheater because I have zero interest in him. He loves calling me a pricktease, then saying he will stick his fingers in parts of my body that draw no attraction for me. Then he tugs and switches to vile. He calls me fat and ugly, although he could not have known the latter as I keep the cam rigidly focused below my neck. *Suck me bitch!* He treats me like shit. I'm technically offended. He's prodding into my personal business where he has no fucking business. What happened to the *Phwoar I want a piece of that!* called out by analogue men on building sites? Part of me is glad I'm being belittled. It absolves me of my scam. And I can pretend what I'm doing is part of some anthropological experiment. It's true I've learnt more about human nature in the past five months than in twenty-eight years. Maybe I should connect him with my therapist to treat his objectification of women. I see Wayne is close so I prepare my best erotic sighs. He cums for a good ten seconds on a voicenote. His gasps turn into a nasal honk, like a Brummie accent, all authentic and deeply unsexy. Then another call, from Kerstin's guy Chris, comes in as a welcome interruption.

I've adapted my routine. I chat late. During the traction of the the first month I got impatient waiting for replies, as if my hovering over the screen made me feel back at work answering consumer complaints. Now with three screens I am beating my path to a world where the customer is not always right. The customers are at my mercy as much as the providers. I file the horny vids and voicenotes and take care to delete mine. Catfishers are ordinary. Anyone peering in from the outside must imagine me as some sort of spotty freak or catwoman unable to achieve meaningful relationships in the real world. But I tried a real-world relationship with Jon and it got me nowhere. Why put up with rows, or suppress resentment about men leaving clothes on my floor or that one who rinsed his cock under my kitchen tap before sneaking back into the night when he thought I was asleep? Kerstin's guy is none of those things. He is both remote and under my manipulation at the same time. My dossier is almost complete before I seal the deal with a meet-up.

Men only want to chat to women around midnight if they want to have sex with her. But there's a pace of flirting that lengthens in direct proportion to the payment an angry partner is willing to pay. The moment his messages and voicenotes turn from the childishly sexual to the borderline romantic, the threshold gets crossed for at least a three-figure fee from an irate woman. Anything less and I'm lucky to get a nice testimonial on the Parsnip site. As my sockpuppets block, ignore, insult or politely decline with a *sorry I have a boyfriend*, my target catfish reels the man in without any question on his part as to her authenticity. I match his tone, delaying *sexy* and *player* replies to a few days after he escalates to the same language. He is the champion, pushing I-wen's, Sandra's or Ellie's boundaries, cucking her supposed Skype fetish fiancé in the US, and insisting on a photographable date in a public place to seal the deal in Biblical terms.

I fall asleep before I can notice the cheap feeling of having Skype sex with men whose profiles I'll have forgotten a week later. Maybe sex on demand with horny men who would otherwise cheat in person or get sucked into cyberporn is a form of public service, worthy of one of the local authority grants I've spent years processing. I feel as though I'm living in a fishbowl of my own creation, with a memory of disposable men approaching goldfish levels. I do my real job before sleeping and put up with my second job bleary-eyed in the office the next morning. I stagger the pace of flirting, then sexting, and escalate to a meeting. I prefer this way. Men want laid-back, uncomplicated women who will call them handsome, pretend they're interesting, and listen to their droning on about gym routines, investments and conspiracy theories. All straight women know this in their soul. In a way I'm taking one for the team. Being cool, never bored, never nagging, for hours on end, is a fair pay-off for the money I get from the wives and girlfriends whose relationship crises I'm fabricating.

Actually hanging around with a date is exhausting. I made the mistake the other night of arriving too early and having to sit at the bar on my own. When he arrived he was already pissed, and his sneaky glances at my cleavage turned lecherous after a chaser. His face was ugly, and I wondered how I had missed this fact when he was flirting on Facebook.

The grubby little bar he arranged confirmed the lack of chemistry. When his hand landed on my thigh on that shitty zebra-skin sofa by the loos, he dug himself an even deeper hole in a too-loud, too-slow voice redolent of five pints.

CATFISH HONEYTRAP

'I love how you're honest in showing off your figure', he slurred. 'As far as I'm concerned you should wear whatever you want'.

I was supposed to find his attitude endearing. I should have batted eyelids or kissed his sweaty cheek. Then I should have asked him to explain more why *Prison Break* was the best drama ever until I ended up naked in his bed in gratitude for his insight. But I opted to leave the moment he went to the loo. I walked into the cold shudder of the night. The pedestrianised street lost its charm on my heels. I couldn't be bothered with work the next day. I'm giving up on real dating.

Kerstin's boyfriend is a joy. In two weeks Chris is in my net. I arrange to meet him at the skin treatment clinic where he works in Fulham. Getting ready to leave the flat takes me twice as long now as before my sleuthing. Then it's two fucking buses and then half-a-mile of walking. I dodge lycra cyclists whizzing along on the riverside path and flap away clumps of gnats hovering ahead of my face. A pair of women jog past me with their polished elbows like fulcrums in symmetry and their arses ticking from side to side. When I finally reach Chris's clinic, it's a non-descript building on the other side of Bishop's Park. I ring the bell and a huge eastern European woman answers the door, bearing one of those permafrowns as if she's stopping me gatecrashing a house-party. I wonder if I've got the wrong building, but then I notice a stack full of surgery and health flyers in the stand behind her. She sees my face and something in her softens. I enter, sign the registration form in my my fake name, and lurk around the mercifully empty waiting room. Despite being overweight, the eastern European woman seems lightfooted as she returns to the reception desk. I glance up at polystyrene tiles, waiting for the moment for the huge woman to look down again. She starts pawing through her handbag. I take half-a-dozen pics, including two I sneak of Chris as he paces past the transparent column in his glass and steel door. I silently will him to slow down and take his time instead of coming out to greet the unknown woman filming him.

I take a four-second vid with a voiceover.

'Sorry, something's come up, so I need to cancel.'

'Okay, so....' The Eastern European returns to her permafrown. She leaves the 'so' just hanging there before returning to her typing.

Next day Chris apologises for missing me, calling me babe three times. I'm tired so I try to get him into a sex chat. But he snaps with a *let's meet up properly*. He has the demeanour of a man not used to being interrupted, like when Jon used to love explaining stuff to me.

'Oh it's a shame babe. I'm horny right now.'

'Save it for me, babe. I need to get back to work now,' he says, as if I'm keeping him from it.

That night he agrees to meet me in the cramped subterranean bar in Vauxhall. I blow £25 on a cabfare. It would mean working almost 2 hours for free tomorrow. But I don't care. All the seats around him are busy, yet he still manages somehow to look alone. His eyes move in shy circles around the entrance, as if wanting to eyeball every woman entering to verify that the date is for real. He looks younger than I had imagined, not quite thirty but also with a scholarly look beyond his years. I get my entry into the bar obscured by the fat bloke in the leather jacket in front of me. The place is cheesy with its neon wall-lighting, exposed brickwork and chrome bar. There's a wasted man propping up a bench against the wall. I take four photos and a four-second vid, and I leave. The texts, photos and vid close the case. I cabfare home and knock back a glass of Chardonnay before I even lay my handbag down. I stretch my arms over my head. I want to rub my tired eyes but I'm still wearing make-up. I flop on my bed and surrender to the calming power of moderate alcohol.

Chapter 6

CONGRATULATIONS! I'VE FOUND PROOF HE IS HAVING AN AFFAIR. Wait, do I just let that message rest? It is lingering on 'Sent' rather than 'Delivered'. Who knows when she will see it? Wait, delete. Stupid woman, why the hell did I open with Congratulations? That's congratulations for me. Two grand in the bank. I unsend the message and write something tenderly professional, without the maniac capitals. I should really have a shorthand for this. Writing *As expected* sounds too brief and final. That would encourage the more selfish clients to take the hint and block me without paying the rest of the bill. *Keeping you in the loop* sounds better. It encourages them to come back for more and doesn't reveal anything of consequence. In the end I decide to personalise it.

'Kerstin, I have some news. Not great, I fear. Shall we chat later?' That sounds like a diagnosis of terminal illness. It's still not quite right, but she takes the bait.

When I Skype her, the awkwardness of the pixel-blurred screen discomforts me. Kerstin is hunched forward over her computer screen, making her chest seem smaller. Her vulnerable, engaging look from our first meeting has changed. This time her blue eyes are glazed over in a way that suggests a quarter-life of disappointments. My attempts to liven the online atmosphere get nowhere. I'm still not perfect at my smiling routine. I'm no good at smiling off-hand, especially when I'm faking empathy. I should have practised with a pocket-mirror beforehand.

'Tell me what it is please, be *pacific*'.

She said the word again, *pa-cif-ic*, loud and clear, as if admonishing me. I could be a bitch and give her peace. Her tone smacks of Estuary Essex and a family background of bling and Range Rovers. I'm relieved to see her drop the Skype cam as a colleague walks past her workdesk. I hear her fat fingers typing her chat. She snivels a tear and writes she needs to get back to work. I'm relieved. I still feel like a novice and was halfexpecting her to poke holes in my story. The next lie is so big and potentially incriminating that I insist on her Skyping me back to hear it from my voice rather than from a text or voicemail.

'He's been chatting to a woman and met her at least twice. We found her workplace and disguised a PI as a cleaner. She found a Post-It note attached to her monitor with her Facebook password on it. We logged on and found the chat and pics'.

Kerstin's snivelling and nodding.

'I followed her to the clinic and the bar. It's case closed. I'm so sorry Kerstin, and sorry you needed my professional services to confirm your suspicions'.

I go out. I want to treat myself. No more cheap edgy buses for me now. No more getting soaked trudging from stop to front door. I feel as though someone has handed me a cheque in exchange for my imagination. Well, the successful seduction is really Fiona's story. But I put my sleuth cleaning lady mark on it, and I'm not getting the benefit of a high-powered transatlantic fiancé. My obsessive mind has become a commodity. I should be a successful writer or artist. This is what being alive is. Most people never push boundaries or adopt the lives of others. The more I work on this project, the more I appreciate how unique it is. I am a digital native. Email is a scourge and Facebook and Skype my champions. I am a modern-day feminist superhero. *Faye Gardner, Catfish Extraordinnaire.*

But no new best friends compete for my attention. I am not suddenly attractive. In fact if the truth about my success came out, I would get ostracised more than when I was a teenager. I'm not missing my old self. I'm like fried onions. I smell better than I taste. Or Fiona's Espresso machine. I am compartmentalising my validation into three manageable screens and three dozen identities. They stay with me in the evenings and all night, humming away like cooperative ghosts. It's time for my call with Brian Marsh. I'm on a high and I need that seeing as he like the rest of the FPIUK are mostly 50-year-old former military men in suits.

'Thanks Jacqueline, it's great to get this chance to speak on the phone.'

The man talking to me is a sober version of the real thing. Fifteen years private investigating experience. Focus on identity theft and financial irregularities. Wants to expand more into infidelity. But so much of this is now online and none of his colleagues are good with social media. And only 6% of his members are women anyway. There's a benign chauvinism in his assumption that only women can investigate infidelity.

'To be frank, Jacqueline, we need someone young and unconventional like you. We're in the second decade of the new millennium but most of my colleagues think it's still 1991.'

'Haha, oh yeah?'

'Yep, we're old farts stuck in the pre-digital age.'

I laugh graciously.

'To be honest Brian I thought your line of work would have a thrill to it. A bit like *Breaking Bad*.'

There's a silence on the end of the line.

'Have you not been watching that?'

'Err, no, I think that one's passed me by. But yeah to be honest most of our line of work involves sitting around in cars for hours waiting for the exact moment for a suspect to leave. A few photos or a pursuit and it's a few minutes of work at the end of a whole day.'

Which sounds a bit like the Mike character in *Breaking Bad*.

'Anyway, Jacqueline I'm glad we had this chat. It's going to be a November meeting at Hazelworth Castle. It's about ten minutes' drive from Boston Spa, just east of Leeds. Keep in touch and see you there!.'

*****

I take the tube to the west end outside of rush hour. Instead of staring at armpits or idiots crammed like sardines poring over their Kindles, I have the luxury of a seat and a view of a dozen case-studies in the carriage. Attractive and plain people collide in my gaze. I notice each parts of their clothing, their trouser lining, their eyeliner applied across their lids. A Home Counties white girl with dreads as thick as cigars. A nerdy thirty-something woman obviously reading something dicey under the outer cover of her Richard Dawkins. A tattoo man straight despite his lycra butt. Nobody turns to meet my stare, so I never need to avert towards looking at nothing. I wonder how many people live like this, bumbling between home and offices and indifferent nights out, jaded and grasping in dead-end jobs and empty existences. As I wait between stations amidst the rubbery gusts of wind I think of my random muses. I could bump into one of them, all of them, get their names pretending to be mistaken identity, adding them to Facebook after my Korean dinner and stirring them into my mire. Maybe this is how novelists or film directors come up with their scripts, scribbling down scenarios and personalities on notepads or Blackberries and ending up with an award-winning film. London in August has the beach feel. The pavement warms up like a promenade and cheatable age men wander the streets in sunglasses and shorts.

When I get to work the next day I lose interest in everything around me. I've kept my hair backcombed three days in a row, too tired to wash it or comb or properly when I'm online till 2 am every night. I take too long downstairs ordering a large coffee and pouring sugar in a thick white fountain before savouring it. I stay in the bathroom for ages. I perfect a semi-dejected walk that conveys that I am always passing by, never stopping or turning around to talk. Even logging on seems a Herculean task. I make some simple mistakes and leave my farty neighbour to correct them. I can't be bothered to take part in the gossip and semi-serious arguments around the water cooler. I am fixated on my catfish profiles, minimizable the moment anyone walks behind me.

    No-one can touch me.

    My computer clock says 4:45 pm. I finish the Bermondsey file and send it for archiving which might as well mean bin. I would stay till 5 just to check on a few profiles. But colleagues are hovering in sight of my screen, so I bide my time another ten minutes to leave at a decent time. As I pop into the Tesco Metro before taking the bus, I find myself queuing one body behind a man I recognise. He has straggly brown hair with hints of early grey at the edges and a Ben Sherman shirt flapping over his slightly bulging waist. As he turns to profile at the till, he senses my stare. He smiles at me in that friendly stranger way that the Kate Winslett character does to Jim Carrey when she's on the checkout in the *Eternal Spotlight of the Spotless Mind*. I recognise him in a second. It's Mike Garner. My eyes meet his and I sense my pupils dilating imploringly. Mike sanely turns back to profile as he bags his eggs and fajitas. I seem to know his posture and mannerisms intimately after three weeks of aimless chatting. I am matching his physical form to the ideal impression I have nurtured in my mind based on our Skype chats and my scrolling through his Facebook posts. I am gasping to speak to him, Mike Garner, this friendly ghost inserted into a human body. But breaking the fourth wall would send my alternative life careering out of orbit. I restrain myself with a growing glow that the man is as sympathetic in the flesh as I've found him online. The boundary between social media and reality has been gloriously punctured for a fleeting moment on my terms.

    When I get home I go to bed early and look him up. After a few minutes my 'hey' turns from 'Delivered' to 'Seen'. We end up texting for an hour. I tell him how anxiety has had its lock on me ever since I was little. He says how he used to get panic attacks, suffering mouthless screams, and sabotaging chances of happiness. He had recurring dreams of being cut off from his anxiety meds and he would wake up in terror.

I want you to know being me coming from an average ass background. I'm a thoroughly average person.

'I know lol'

I think you're all nuts. Women I mean

'Uh oh. Chauvinist alert lol'.

Yeah like you. Won't even show me your face. Like you're Asian in the south sense wearing a headscarf or something.

'Wouldn't that be a burka lol?'

Oh yeah. Maybe. Don't know.

'You can see my lovely foot though'. I pan my Skype lens towards my right foot.

Lovely foot. Where's the other one? X

'What if I've only got one?'

Haha for real.

'Yeah for real. You're for real Mike'.

Haha I'm for real. With my ex whenever I was in full control and standoffish she absolutely wanted me.

'that's some shit testing she was doing then, poor you lol'

Haha yeah. And the minute I relied on her and loved her she didn't want me

'Mmhmm'.

I'm the most loving person in the world. But also the most anxious.

I feel myself smiling. If I let him Skype my Caucasian face he would see my eyes like saucers.

Need someone to help push me but it's hard when you're alone doing it ngl

'It's your parents Mike. It always begins there. They screw you up for life'.

Yeah for real. My mum's lesbian. She cheated on my dad. He walked out when I was little and she was in a relationship with a woman for the next 14 years.

CATFISH HONEYTRAP

Mike's open sincerity is blurring my world. I can't use any of this material for any Ian or ex-con catfish chat. I can't see how a middleaged lesbian can honeytrap anyone. I wonder if grandfather Bartholomew knew about these shenanigans in leafy Cheshire.

'She wasn't lesbian then.'

My cocky reply is left on 'Seen'. He's obviously not in the mood for levity. Either that or my casual use of 'then' is confusing him about whether I mean historical time or logical progression.

'Just had enough of men for a while lol'. I might as well keep digging.

It's a very confusing world for me. Before I moved down south I always lived with my mum. I think I've never had a male role model in my life.

I exhale and press my cheek into my elbowed palm. Maybe my connecting incognito with Mike is good karma for all the shit I'm pulling with everybody else.

'It sucks Mike. Just making some food'.

Wait. I-wen. I don't want you to go.

'Oh. Here I am. Not going anywhere. I'm knackered'.

His texts switch to a voicenote. *No, I-wen, I mean, I was just wondering.* His voice sounds all small and hopeless at odds with the confident smiler I saw at the Tesco. *Would you come over and hang out with me?*

'Oh'.

Not to hook up. I just don't want to be alone right now.

I almost laugh. But there's a heavy feeling in my throat. But a *please* is not going to make me feel differently.

'Sorry, my friend is coming over', I lie. Being bashful and delicate is the East Asian culture I am appropriating.

I never expected to feel humbled by the power of emotional manipulation I am exerting. I could bury everything now. I could bank the ten grand I've made and deposit my way to a decent flat somewhere in zone 3. All my faking could stay buried in the back of my mind. It wouldn't resurface unless I go back to a therapy session.

I have a sinking feeling in my stomach. I'm going to do something, just not that. But I'm done with stalking bitchface. Hatescrolling through her interior design posts and her pics with Jon no longer holds holds the allure it had over me. I take a last look at her Facebook and see her standing on a leafy street somewhere with Jon hugging her from behind. Her smile is frozen to her face, and the whiteness in her eyes makes her look frightened. Or maybe I'm projecting onto her. I don't block her. I can't since I was never her friend. But I'm not stalking her again. I'm a professional now. Besides, I know I have no right to interfere with the happy couple. Hoi is more victim than perpetrator. I text Fiona to tell her my resolution: 'I'm not stalking bitchface Hoi anymore x'.

Fiona replies quite fast, considering how much she's been ignoring me recently.

Oh, wow, did she block you hun? x

Ugh. I suppose it's too much to expect her to see the good in me after her accusations last month. I'm aware of them both without any further stalking. Jon deleted his Facebook account but he's still appearing in Hoi's pics. Like his old email account he will have closed it and probably re-opened a new profile with filters.

'No, we were never added remember? I'm just over it all now. Do me a favour Fiona and delete her from your Facebook.'

I'm a professional now. I'm over Jon. I'm channelling his cheating vicariously via Mike and mystery man Marco. Their manspeak informs my chatting when I channel the Eminem-lookalike as the DMs pile in. Two of his latest DMs are from gays. *Nice. You're a 10*, says fellow muscleman Ed Johnson.

'Fiona, can you delete her please?'

Oh yeah sure hun x

Chapter 7

I don't know what it's like for anyone else, not that I know anyone else in my position, but the moment the real world collides with the fake is not an eye-rolling *told you so* but a warning that my professional career is over. Somehow I've fucked up. I'm checking on I-wen Tai's Facebook page. She's uploaded a photo of herself outside the London Dungeons. At the top of the list of likes and hearts is one from MnM. For the life of me I can't work out the chances of my best female and best male catfish targets knowing each other online. Maybe there's an algorithm that transmits to third parties somehow, given the amount of time I've spent lurking on both their accounts from multiple log-ins. I'm feeling a dizzy sort of seasick. Like when you're waiting on a train at Clapham Junction and you get startled thinking it's moving because the train on the other platform is pulling away.

I should have hidden more friends lists. Maybe I-wen was like me weeks ago, searching clicking on random friends of friends until she found the handsome ex-con. I've been messaging MnM from my real account for days, and I'm pissed off that my muse of all people should get in the way. I suppose there's little harm his heart can do. My fake MnM account gets random DMs from women almost every day, even married ones (kerching!). The poor man can't get intimate with all of them. He accepted my add from my real account last week. There's nothing in our limited *sup?* exchange on Messenger so far to suggest that he suspects being targeted for catfishing.

Maybe the Taiwan woman is lonely and she was messaging MnM at random. I should ask Fiona for advice. But she is bristling at my refusal to delete those three accounts and I don't want to offload real online feelings into her. I haven't seen her in a week or spoken to her in three days. Even her texts have become brief and unrevealing, as if I've faded into the peripheral world of catfish who take themselves too seriously.

But my sanctity is tarnished. Normally when I get home from work, the screenworld is my reset. I'm a fish returned to water. But now my targets are slipping out of my control.

I stalk MnM's posts. His few pics say enough. His personality revolves around the barbed wire tattoo around his bicep and his protein shakes. I ambush him on Messenger and the pause in his snappy replies and short dots for writing imply that he is put out. But then his emojis offer me relief. He lets on about his background. He was a minder, then an enforcer. Images enter my mind of nightclubs, or private security. Then he shows me a scar and I think of fingers being broken and eyes being gouged out. Why the hell can't I be interested in a decent man? Why didn't I get the number of Fiona's microfinance friend helping coffee growers in Vietnam or wherever it was?

What do you do darling, he messages.

'Oh, I'm a writer', I lie.

Nice, he replies. Then he sends me a selfie next to a mirror in what looks like a toilet in a bar.

'You're fit', I reply.

I am. I give the best hugs. Bet you want one now.

I do want a hug. But do I also want his violent world in my life?

'I'm sure you've got plenty of women to hug'.

Nope. I want just one to hug. I want peace.

Smouldering sincerity and a six-pack. Nice.

'Oh yeah? You've been through a lot of stuff then?'

Bad upbringing does that to people lol. Seen too much shit

He sends me a heart emoji and a *sorry gotta go now babe*.

A final check on Ellie before bed. There's a message from wanker Wayne. *Isn't ghosting me out of order? I made you cum three times.* I didn't cum three times. I didn't cum once. I check PayPal. His girlfriend has paid me only half. But I can't face honk-nosed Wayne again. I message him 'Sorry Wayne, Arun's come over from New York. Surprise visit. He saw our chats and he told me to end all contact with you'. I block him and get to bed.

I close my eyes and let out a heavy sigh. I am stuck between selfindulgence and enlightenment. I have been cutting back on my own erotic thrill. But on nights like these when I'm bored and lonely, most nights like these, This MnM guy livens me up, or at least distracts me from the nuts and bolts of PI work. *I deserve my pleasure*, I think to myself. He's my bit of online rough to balance civilised Marco Prendergast. I lay down with my smartphone and scroll through his tattoo pics. Two unattainable men are my options. Tonight is Marco night. I slip my jeans down and press my hand and wrist between my legs. I see his gym pic showing his lats bearing a tatoo up his spine. I would love him to chat to me now. The pretentious handsome twat snaps me out of my repetitive *hey babys* and *show me your faces*. If Marco were a landscape, he would be the Dolomites, rugged, presentable, and barely accessible. My catfish honeytraps would be Leicestershire, flat, boring and predictable. There's a quota for boredom which I exceeded long ago. Marco is my human black box right now.

Euuurgh. Am I falling for him? I hate clichés. This isn't a love story. Marco could be a balding forty-year-old in his mum's basement for all I know. Like me he never shows his face. It's not impossible that he's been photoshopping pics, or even catfishing attractive men to get me going. But it would take a male version of me to get a man to send a shower video. I scroll some more through the pics of the man who is 99% likely to be real. Then sleepiness overtakes me.

*****

After three months and three dozen profiles I gain compassion for my online creations. Doesn't my frumpy Caitlin deserve a little love? She got ghosted. I feel a sense of righteous communion. They get dumped, bruised and belittled as my own flesh and blood. Why the hell is it called ghosting? She doesn't really exist and never met these guys and can't haunt them like Cathy at her window. Anything I play along with in my chat is going to sound like an insult. And yet staying quiet at this guy's stupid comments would lend my sockpuppet a scrap of dignity ridiculous from top to bottom. But then it's all fine. Some of my creations are clingier, more pathetic than others. Clingy Caitlin is working a treat on wedding-list Damon. Her desperate hearts on his posts cast I-wen in a self-respecting light. It gives Damon a topic of conversation and a thrill to push her boundaries.

My creations are living life backwards. Normally behind every Linkedin, Facebook or Twitter there's a human with a job, a mortgage and a life. My puppets are flipped. But as I inhabit their worlds I find it hard to keep my own diminished life segregated from them. They don't have personalities, feelings or thoughts, except the ones I give them. They don't fight, harbour dangerous thoughts or bear grudges.

They are my lightning rods waiting for my plot. Smiling strangers want to speak to them. I am living my social life through them. Sometimes I leave accounts dormant for a week or so before posting some link or photo extracted from my reserve files. Like newly-washed windows they dazzle onlookers accustomed to the build-up of grime. The brightness of a selfie or random London pic are a visual jolt that elicits hungry *hey babes*.

Nothing separates me from my triumvirate of three computers and my ergonomic IKEA chair. My body glides between screens and my files. I know each individual under each alphabetised card. I have plucked four dozen humans from humdrum lives. I am convinced I am the only person in the world doing this. The more time I spend time fielding responses to my creations, the more I understand human nature. I am above the law. Some days, when I match morning email requests with Facebook adds by the evening, I feel like God.

I'm getting more hits with my Eminem-lookalike con. Jade is taking the bait. Opening with a 'what's your jam?' is irresistible to women ten years older than me.

CATFISH HONEYTRAP

Okay well I've got a three month old baby now and a seven year old. Still single. However I think I'm not for you.

'Why not? You're sexy babe'.

Well I'm a benefits mother. I had a career but at 37 decided on another child.

Right man hasn't appeared for me. X

A single mum. I should channel some masculine arsehole energy. The Eminem-lookalike is so handsome he could get away with anything. (*Single mum, two kids? No thanks! Three times as many people to disappoint lol*). But before I reply I hear some shouting outside. I look down from my sash window and I see one of the men from the top floor. I pull my curtains and go back to Jade. She's messaged again.

What's your age, job and living situation? Car etc?

It's a shame Jade doesn't have a jealous husband, too. A father of two would pay me more in the hope of making a divorce process less protracted. Another DM comes in. This one actually is married. She says she needs a PT. His muscly, but not too muscly, build, must be working magic on fat housewives looking to lose a few pounds. But before I can scroll down to reply, Vicky has blocked herself.

*****

There's a scary-looking woman called Leonie in my I-wen DM. She's got a blonde chav bun that's had all its colour bleached out. She looks hard and threatening.

Hi just a question how do you know Marco Prendergast?

She looks like the least likely person to be in Marco's circle. I should ignore her brazen intrusion into the fun part of my fake life.

'oh that was ages ago', I type back, sensing that my power of anonymity has gone. I hold my breath in foreboding as the infamous three dots appear.

What was ages ago?

I've been in these exchanges so many times before that I should really have a prepared script.
I'm asking how do you know him?
'I liked some of his posts on Japanese culture and we got chatting', I lie.
My reply is Seen instantly. Leonie is silent.
What? I'm asking how u know him
'thats how I know him'. I can write ungrammatically, too, bitch. Does she seriously expect a catfish sleuth CEO to waste a lie on her? Object, people, activities. They're all my concern to make things run smoothly.
are you talking to him now?
It's odd that she doesn't say 'seeing'. She's rumbled my game.
'No but we got on really well'
Make it make sense. I wanna know how you know him. You've just said you liked his stuff and you ended up talking? So I'll ask you again. How do you know him?
Screw her. Can't a catfish extraordinnaire have at least one fake relationship for real? I log into see Marco. He's offline but he's sent me half-a-dozen 'thinking of you pics'. There's a bicep crunch, shower pics and a model-like pose he has done in black-and-white. He's laying naked on white bedsheets with one leg open and his hard-on propping at his six-pack. More than anything I want to see his face. But part of me enjoys his manipulation over me. It's payback for my months of fakeness. There's an unspoken understanding that he does not want to be easily contacted by me. We have bursts of intense chat and exchanges of faceless pics. I pretend our chats are unplanned. He has no way of knowing that I will drop my catfish work for the chance of ten minutes of unpaid flirting with him.

The chavbun woman has made me tense with her fight-or-flight abuse and I'm going to relieve it. I lay back and hold his model photo right above my face. I masturbate frantically. At first I have to force the pleasure. Marco's not here to talk me through and chavbun ran my blood cold. But my pleasure builds as I look in hope for Marco to some online. I focus on his groin and feel the crest coming. By the time I'm done my phone hand has gone chilled with gentle pins and needles.

*****

I'm going shopping and for the first time I feel like a tourist in my own town. It feels weird, realising that I am looking at people differently. The familiarity of South London appeals to me as I project imaginary scenarios onto the people walking past. Strangers in the flesh become candidates for entrapment the moment I choose to eavesdrop on a man saying his name at a bank counter or a woman shouting an unusual name across the street. I make mental notes of half-a-dozen relationship crises as I enter Zara. I walk around, touching summer dresses, awaiting some enchantment to grip me, and jot down the names in the notebook in my handbag. I shorthand a few clues about opening gambits (*sorry are you Helen's brother who was in Zara earlier?*).

As I daydream possibilities on my way to the book shop, my online muse catches up with me. I scrunch my eyes. Opening them again she is still there. My online fakery has become real. Her fat butt has appeared from nowhere. I speed up my walk, pretending to want to reach the non-fiction end of the bookstore. But she is matching my pace. My heart is racing as my walking pace is turning me into a parallel stalker. Is it OK to follow people in real life? Two tables separate us as I overtake her. As I glance to my right, part of me hopes it isn't her, or that she was a trick of my imagination. She takes a right turn and makes for the stairwell. But it *must* be her. She even has that confident yet slovenly wiggle of her arse as she walks. She's probably going for a croissant in the café section. But then I remember the coffee shop is on the ground floor behind me. As I exit into the cobbled square I see her walking across the glass footbridge to the Primark opposite.

I'm going straight home. I can't bring myself to follow her. It's hard enough leading multiple lives on Facebook without losing my mind chasing a chubby apparition all along the high street. In any case she had a rushed look of someone desperate to buy a relative a gift before closing time. I walk down the passageway to the bus station and my path is blocked by a woman with a large pushchair misbalanced by an overfilled Tesco carrier bag. She has a Nokia phone in one hand and is struggling with a child kicking its limbs in the other. For a moment it seems like a ploy to block my path, as though I-wen/Jos is about to jump me from behind. But she places the toddler deftly in his chair and pushes to the side, no longer obliging people to part their ways around her.

I brisk past her and take a left down a short alley hosting an emergency exit at the base of a steel staircase. I lean against the wall and unzip my coat and flap it open. I let the breeze ricocheting into the alley chill the sweat which I've built up on my neck and under my arms. In my chest my heart returns to normal beat. My knees stop wobbling and I resist the urge to crouch in a time-out on the ground.

I board the bus and all the other passengers have their heads down, their shoulders low, with everyone looking under thirty glued to their phones. My physical encounter with my catfish target makes a mockery of my immersive virtual world. I am echoed by my fellow almostmature creatures, all slumped over screens and unsmiling. When I get home, I open my DMs. A shudder passes down my spine, like a delayed reaction to the fright outside Primark. A thank you and a tear from another woman whose cheating boyfriend I have exposed. I send back an airhug GIF. I check PayPal. I've made another grand. Jon would have been so proud, if he had stuck around. He loved to pity me on my deadend job and impress me with his very important career. But I've gone from Primark to Prada and he'll never know.

I treat myself to takeaway pizza to celebrate. I want to chat to Marco but he's offline. Last night we chatted for an hour and he called me BBC. I searched the acronyms and found big black cock and Britishborn Chinese. Then he said it was because I was classy. So the not-quite compliment turned into a proper one and I dozed off in my warm glow. But tonight he's busy. I scroll through Amazon and make three random orders before cancelling them. I devour the IKEA catalogue and look up DIY men who erect furniture for a fee. I can treat myself now. But as I take a third bite of the Hawaian pizza my stomach revolts. I could talk to Fiona. But a chat with her in real life would be too much. She would want to speak honestly. I would feel all protected by her. I'm not ready to come clean about how I really feel. Besides, she's a noisy eater. I actually hear the slap of her tongue off the roof of her mouth, and a slab of pizza makes no difference.

*****

The next day it's my appraisal time with Aparajita. Harry's temp replacement sitting next to me is making me a bit nervous. He has a weird habit of sitting bolt upright before clapping his hands together like a toddler applauding something only he finds funny. I haven't been to the HR room since my interview and it takes me a couple of wrong turns to find it. Shiny doorknobs stick out. Like eyes, they are watching me. Aparajita is going to eat into my lunch routine of ten minutes with Tupperware and fifty with my catfish. I knock on her door and find her inside wearing the same blue eyeliner I remember from when she hired me. There are flowers in a vase on the desk next to a box of tissues and I wonder if she put those there on purpose. Everyone thinks she's incredibly annoying. Sympathetic people tend to be. As I sit down I tuck the falling strands of my hair behind my ears. I washed my hair two days ago, so it's not greasy. I can't refuse a coffee because she insists it's an informal 'touching base' chat.

'Oh, hi there', Aparajita says, with an uplifted tone indicating pleasant surprise as opposed to the same old predictable bi-annual routine. As I sit down she crosses one leg over the other. She's wearing a dark pantsuit with naff high heels on her feet.

'Hi'.

'How are you *feeling*?'

Feel! Feel! Feel! Feelings threaten to interrupt my wellbeing. I always felt that if I kept my head down at work and just got on, I would escape getting my base touched or cascaded down. I push myself up on the chair, feeling the gentle breeze from Aparajita's fan. It's too comforting, luring me in.

'How's the social media marketing coming along? Look, it's a big challenge. Don't feel embarrassed to shout out or ask for help'.

Aparajita is far too fragile to be having coffee with me. If only she knew the truth about my motivations, my half-arsed work at the office, my hiding in the toilet for half an hour each morning to sit out my hangovers. The fact that I spend half my work time developing catfish profiles and that nobody glancing my screen would be any wiser. I could crush her touchy-feely passive aggression in an instant. If I were a man they would be winking at my success. I would be on *Dragon's Den* winning offers to invest in the PI business. Right now I can't stand to look into Aparajita's endearing brown eyes and her heavy eyeliner any more than is absolutely necessary. I'm the absolute opposite of what she takes me for. So, no, I'm not asking for help, or *engaging* with her to get more *focused*. She needs to take a hint.

'I know this brave new online world can seem a bit crazy for women of our age'.

Did she actually just say that? Poor woman. She is leaning left in her swivel chair like an A-Level drama teacher trying to connect with a teenage student. She's over forty, well forty at least. I've never seen her CV but she has to be at least ten years older than me. Anyway. Time to put on my mask.

'Oh well, it's a slow start but I'm enjoying the independent work'.

CATFISH HONEYTRAP

'You know things are tight now, what with all the local authority cuts. We need to make sure everyone's playing to their strengths.' She says it with that fake-sounding upward inflection, as if trying to sound sensitive. Her brown-eyed stare seems to have glazed over.

'Yeah, I suppose. What with Harry being let go I suppose we're already cutting back'.

'Oh Harry went of his own accord. Got a new position in a non-profit'.

'Oh. Well we've both been so busy he never told me much about it'. Aparajita's blue eye-liner stare does not break.

'Well, anyway, I don't mind staying later today to finish the Haringey file'.

'Oh, I don't think you staying late makes much difference', Aparajita replies with a forced smile. She does not add the words 'any more', but I hear them hanging in the air. As I turn to leave she pulls a Colombo on me.

'By the way, one more thing Faye'. Aparajita is sitting upright now. 'It's been brought to my attention that you've been using the internet for personal use during office hours'.

'Oh'.

'Sorry, we're all human but things are really tight right now. The powers that be are holding us to the no personal emailing or browsing policy.

That includes internet dating I'm afraid'.

I am about to scoff in laughter but manage to suppress it. She starts jabbing her finger on her Ipad, something she does whenever she wants to signal that she's finished talking with me. A big part of me wants to scream *fire me then*. But there's always a chance my sleuthing could dry up. Aparajita turns her gaze back to her screen, her high heels back on the floor as if rooting her while she types rapidly.

I get back to my desk. I feel less nervous with toddler temp now that I've practised leaving and returning to my workstation without him degenerating into a clapping fit. I don't want to take this job more seriously but I know I need to throw Aparajita off the scent. Nobody wants a colleague who spends all day hooked to her computer but only ever gets the bare minimum done. I google local authority and marketing job vacancies, and leave results in my browser history. I download my old CV and write out some jobsearch questions on a separate piece of paper: *What are my key skills? What are my weaknesses?* and leave both visible on the screen before going to the loo. Before leaving for home I make sure to print out a copy and leave it on top of the clutter of papers accumulating on my desk.

It's just past 2pm and I'm going to take a retrospective half-day off because Philip's messaged saying Anastasia is making an excuse to go to Lewisham. The building site there is where she's been cheating seeing her Bulgarian lover. Taking the half-day off work will spare me the farts the temp in the cubicle next to me will be doing that smell like the curry he just finished. I already checked the building site on Google Street view. I scrolled up and down the street after I saw the image capture was from only 2 months ago. I move the cursor up and down the street, looking for some casual sign of Anastasia. But scrolling a few clicks away takes me to a T-junction and back in time to images from over a year ago. The old buildings are still undemolished and Anastasia was not in the country then. But I scroll up and down anyway.

I tell the taxi driver to stop two streets down. I don't want anyone to know exactly where I'm going. I have grown the second skin of a detective. I walk down a backstreet and realise that I'm a bit early and will soon look like a loiterer. There's a constant heavy drone of traffic and the din of occasional exiting the multistorey carpark to my left. Ahead there is a small demolition site presumably about to replaced with some microflats. There's a clanging of metal and drills. One of the workmen winds down the window in his van and lights a cigarette. It seems to burn down quickly, like when Fiona smokes. He tosses the butt through the gap in the window. It catches a sudden gust of wind and flies exoneratingly down the street. Then I check my phone. Philip has messaged to confirm that she should be here about now. Then I see her. Her monobrow and peroxide hair are raised a few inches by her high heels. For some reason she's holding a folder as she does a jolting walk down the street in her heels. She looks like a bling version of the estate agent I dildo-bombed back in April.

A man exits a van on the wrong side for my camera. Happily he walks to the end of the Ford Transit and raises his arm to hug Anastasia. I take four pics, including one with them kissing. Anastasia has an avocadoshaped sweat on the small of her back that betrays too much rushing around in the heat. I'm about to turn to head back when the woman sees me looking. She locks eyes on me. I'm looking back and she doesn't feel the need to look away. There's no nod or smile coming from her. But I see a sort of cynical acknowledgement in her. It's like she's sussed me out in the same time it took me to click my camera.

I forward the pics to Philip and voicenote him my condolences. Knowing the grand in payment is happily on its way I treat myself to a cab home. When I get back to my bedsit it's *Grand Designs* time and Kevin McCloud is going to make everything right. I google 'what do to if you get fired'. The first response is 'Rejoice'. I log into I-wen and find some likes from Marco on her profile. He sends me an update of his holistic lifestyle. *I just finished taikiken ritsuzen meditation and I'm about to take a cold shower. Now about to make my brain go on fire with Etterna.*

'Do you win some sort of prize for doing that?', I reply, adding an amazement emoji.

You know it babe.

'I hope the water puts out your brain'. That comment was lame. I don't want there to be too long a silence between us. Silence is fine as long as one of us is using our device, one of us typing and the other seeing the dots. I have to keep the communication constant or our intimacy will elapse. But the reason for his standoff becomes clear.

He replies with a pic of his muscly arm holding up three different showergels. He's naked in the shower. It's just enough to escalate the tension without being as trashy as a dickpic. All this time chatting and we've never seen each other's faces. I reply to one with a shy emoji. The buzz of playing hard to get is as good as a glass of wine. Hours of flirting pass by as I abolish all my sense of time as well as space. I end up inhabiting Fiona's world. I, too, am in a long-distance relationship and trying to stay good. And Marco believes me.

'All this time chatting and I've been ignoring my fiancé.'

Aaahh go on girl haha when's he back? X

'Oh, he spends half the year out there'. I'm adopting Fiona's transatlantic lifestyle like it's second nature.

That's good then. I've done a long distance before and it was impossible to maintain. Your friend cool with it too?

'Oh yeah. What was it like?'

I got time, talk as much as you want haha sometimes what you need is the opposite of what you want, and clearly those guys couldn't see a good thing if it hit them in the face.

I could never land a man like this in real life. But a chubby East Asian catfish is working her magic.

Yeah it's easy to rush based on attractions, you found things in common with this guy. He's called Arun, right?

'Yeah, he's handsome, ambitious. Worth waiting around for. He's not a player'.

I'm not a player either. I don't have relationships.

Golden words of a player.

With me being in 2 different countries throughout the year it just causes trust issues and I'm always hella busy with work so haven't got the time a woman would deserve in a relationship either so I've always been honest about it and said it's just sex and hanging out so no one gets hurts, guess you could call that a player but everyone needs sex, you been behaving yourself for 3 months then or having fun?

CATFISH HONEYTRAP

He is a window on a lifestyle I want. I can almost copy and paste his spiel into Ian's gambits, or to the DMs the Eminem lookalike is getting.

'Behaving, yeah. Just waiting for my tall mystery man to sweep me off my feet'.

Well I'm 6ft 2 and very strong so I'm definitely assertive. But when I'm in I like to go hard and a small woman would definitely feel it.

'I'm not just small. I'm fat too'. I reply with a crying emoji. Am I really into him? Or is this just smooth-talk research for my Eminem profile?

Shut up you're gorgeous with or without extra weight. Curvy girls are hotter anyway. If you ever want to send pics, sending a pic is a lot less stress than fingering yourself in a webcam.

I gasp at his tone switching from flirty to pornographic. I should be taking notes for my Eminem flirt with Jade.

I'm glad you've only ever known me to be on semen retention. It means im in incredible self control. As must men cannot even control their lust for a week.

Of course. He can't just be any other sexy professional guy. He has to be a sensei, obsessed with holy no-wankiness.

'I'm impressed. I like talking to you Marco'.

Me too. Can I tell you a secret?

'Go ahead'.

I know this is a fake account. I'm not mad though. I've had fun and I've known from the start. I still think you're awesome and we get on great. You still there? Can I see you at last? Quit playing, let me see your face.

I've been in this scenario dozens of time before. It always ends the same. I either block before I can get blocked, or I turn the accusation back onto the man and mute his messages. But they were my targets. Marco is different. I like him and want to pursue this further. It's time to drop my guard.

'Actually Marco, I have a confession. All the time I was being Skyped by my fiancé. He's in New York. I climaxed with you and let him think he was getting me off'.
Accusation evaded. Subject changed. Tension released.
I log out of my chat with Marco and log into Ian. The hours hanging with a man has masculinised my brain. I need to harness the male gaze.
I check on relationship crisis Lizzie. She's online.
'Strawberry?', I type. It's been two months since I asked her about her jam.
My message is seen right away. She replies with a question mark.
'Raspberry?'
Blackcurrant you fake ass cunt lol
This person is not contactable on Messenger.

*****

I need to detox. Hours spent staring at screens is warping my sense of reality. It's 3pm, which means I've been online with Marco for three hours. I need to get out of Dodge, as Fiona's guy would say.
Fancy hanging out, hun? x
It's the first text from Fiona two hours ago. I haven't checked my phone all day. Then there was a second text ten minutes later: *Come on, Faye, it's my day off and Aaron's been ignoring me all day.*
I do feel like getting some sunshine. But before I text a reply I check Fiona's Facebook page. She's just posted a couple of pics of her and some of her skinny Marketing friends from a Mexican food festival at St Pancras. There's a lanyard above a taco stall saying 'Bicentenario'.
I don't want to tag along but I do want to go out.
Sorry I was busy but will come and knock on your door now, I text her disingenuously, since Fiona's taco pic from central London was posted 2 minutes ago. I switch the detective agency phoneline to voicemail. I stand up with a spring twanging from my chair: handbag, phone,

travelcard. I'm heading away from Fiona. in a different direction, to visit a country pub outside Orpington where Jon once took me. I'm finishing some Summer wedding list business at the same time. The journey through south-east London takes me down treeless roads bristling with take-away litter, some teenagers on bikes shouting out of earshot, and two bald men in St George's shirts. My phone is wedged at the bottom of my handbag and set to Vibrate.

Zone 6 gives way to some greenery and then the road where I need to get off to post printed-out Messenger chats, emails and pics. They're for Elaine, a middle-aged client in Bedfordshire who was on Summer's wedding list. She seems suspicious of my online-only work. Her 50year-old husband keeps travelling and I keep her custom by pretending I have a mobile team onto him. I post her the evidence from the Orpington sorting office in order to gain a different postmark on the envelope.

My envelope is so stuffed with timed details of husband Roger's movements that I need to get it weighed. It should have taken a minute but there's a queue being held up at the counter by some by some bald geezer paying for a book of stamps with what look like his takings from a penny arcade. I reach the till and my bulging envelope full of halfreal, half-fake details weigh in at 300 grammes. All those *7:23 pm Roger enters Travelodge, 9:35 am cleaner finds evidence that he shared his bed* entries are starting their way to a Bedfordshire village as I walk out to get my own slice of rural life.

I feel refreshed on my walk to the gastropub. As it looms into sight a *Baby on Board* sticker peers at me from the back window of one of the parked cars by the front entrance. Around me the grass has all been bailed and stacked. The stubble in the field is turning yellow. A warm breeze carries the faintest whiff of nature, of reality, to my nostrils. My back is gently buffeted by the wind. As I sit outside I'm basking in this rare excursion out of the city and bask in the offline world like an old coat. As I sip my cider some kids run across the grass in front of my bench. There are real people, real families. There's no laptop, no Ipad, in sight, and only a few smartphones. I am a human cog like the others, going round and round. I have become a functioning part of the world. I refrain from taking random pics of wine glasses, sunshine, and my painted nails. My catfish image bank can rest. When the early evening shade encroaches on my table I move inside. They still have the lamb tagine on the menu from the last time with Jon.

I know this truce cannot last. The pace inside is only a bit slower than zone 4. It should be dialled down a few notches, like in a Richard Curtis film. The man sitting at the table next to me looks mid-forties, balding and wearing a buttoned-down Hawaiian kind of shirt. His wife just spent a minute checking text messages before going to the toilet. She looks a few years older. But her figure is good in high-waisted jeans and a crop-top showing her tits haven't sagged with age. She looks too attractive for him. But I know this won't stop him.

'Lamb roast for Joe?'. A lanky waiter with a huge Adam's apple barely out of teenage years is bringing an order in my direction.

'Yes, I'm Jo', I lie. 'I ordered the lamb'.

The gangly barman looks confused. He probably remembers I ordered the tagine. Maybe he's calculating if it's worth his minimum wage job to correct me or just to dump the plate in front of me.

'Err, sorry, if it's the roast, it's mine', mystery Joe says with a smile.

'Oh, but I'm Jo? Oh. Sorry I ordered the tagine'.

The Adam's Apple man plonks the dish on his table.

'You're Joe, too? What are the chances?'.

'Small world', I giggle and flip my hair. 'Your surname's not Thompson, is it? It'd be nice to find a relation'.

'Haha, sorry love, it's Schmitt.'

'Schmitt? German?'

'Austrian actually. Granddad. Long story love'.

'Oh nice. Sounds more interesting than coming from Streatham!'

'Aaaw, Streatham's lovely. I used to work there years back'.

CATFISH HONEYTRAP

His wife is coming back from the toilet. She'll take a few seconds to walk round the bar to see her husband chatting to a woman on her own.

'Well enjoy the roast. Let me know what it's like. I was torn between that and the tagine'.

I look around innocently. There's an enormous flat-screen TV fixed to the wall above an empty-woodburning stove. I glance back to the happy couple and catch a sight of his wife straighten her blouse with a supercilious air. Joe Schmitt is sitting back with his hands in his pockets. For a split second before he senses that I'm glancing in his direction, his profile expression looks strange. Like he's trying to work out the answer to a puzzle.

*****

My online world is drawing me back into the city. It's almost dusk when I leave for the bus stop. A fox darts in front of me. Either it isn't bothered by my presence or it doesn't see me. I resume my pace and the fox doesn't move. It remains stock still with its head cocked, licking a leaf on a bush next to a dustbin. As a car goes past the fox glances at me before disappearing into the gloomy greenery. I walk to the gap in the foliage where the animal vanished and a sudden breeze carries to my nose the fresh scent of gorgeously moist autumn. I peer through the leaves and spot a flagpole and an invasion from the newbuilds. A moist leaf brushes my right cheek.

As I walk to my bus stop a happy-looking couple walk arm-in-arm to the pub I've just left. The woman is pregnant. I feel like a leftover woman in Hoi's Chinese culture. My womb will not keep kids an option for many years longer. I'm neither married with kids, nor am I a successful career woman. Except I am, but I'm like a secret agent. I can't tell anyone what I do without tearing the online house down around me. I wonder what Jon is doing now, maybe shopping at Fortnum and Mason, or buying a pregnancy kit for Hoi's successful conception.

Chapter 8

The next morning PayPal confirms I've made a grand in a day. My head feels dizzy all morning. Part of me is expecting impossible congratulations to trickle in from my dozens of targets. I want to scream at someone in triumph. But there's nobody. But I deserve for things to change. When I see the email in my work inbox about a plan to make redundancies, I decide to take action. I get the earlier bus and there's twenty minutes or so to kill in the Costa opposite. Half of that is getting taken up by a new pink-haired staff member who's making a galacial pace taking orders and who seemed out of her depth just now when I assured her I wanted milk in my cappuccino. *Oh, you mean natural milk?* Yes, milk milk. Actually getting up to the office late will give me an edge. Aparajita wil be safely settled in her office to hear me give notice and nobody else will remark my lateness after all these months of the same.

The lift is empty as I ascend to the eighth floor. All my best-laid plans of using the stairs several times a day to lose weight will come to nothing now. As I enter our room Aparajita is mincing her way in front of me holding an empty coffee jug.

'Hi Faye. Sorry have you got a moment?'

'Sure'. The sober tone of her question has shifted the one of things in the air.

As I follow her into her office she takes her seat officiously, and motions me to sit down in front of her. I hope this is not going to be another *how are you feeling?* session followed by another passive-aggressive offer to relieve me of the social media strategy tasks.

'Thanks Faye. Sorry to have to say this, but I wanted to make this a verbal before you receive the written confirmation letter later today.'

This sounds ambivalent. I don't think I've ever received a written confirmation since I got a mititgating circumstances award back in my

CATFISH HONEYTRAP

Bristol uni days giving me an extra week to submit coursework for my panic attacks.

'Yes, I'm sorry that you've been reported for breaking council policy again. Colleagues have noticed you using the internet for personal uses during office hours.'

Oh. How feeble she sounds now. Personal uses indeed. It's been more like this job has turned into a personal hobby to facilitate my real career.

She has a dead-eyed stare, bereft of interest or understanding.

'I'm afraid that Myspace is in no way connected to your job profile here.'

Myspace! Like it's 2005. It makes sense. Aparajita thinks she's still young. Like Fiona she tries too hard, always imagining herself five years younger.

'I know it's not nice to be reprimanded but as you know we have a three strikes policy. I'm afraid if it happens again, we have grounds for dismissal. This is why I need to move you away from the social media role and back onto grants ...'

'Actually Aparajita', I pause and see her tired-looking mascara eyes return my stare. A few possible responses flash through my mind. None of them points to me wanting to stay in my job. I could reveal the truth to her, just to see her condescending Romford Barratt home smirk fall off her face. But deep down I know I'm the pathetic one here. My sixfigure success needs to stay a dirty secret.

'I think I'm going to have to hand in my notice.' I'm impressed by the polished and slightly smarmy tone I say these words. It's nice for her to hear a dose of her own medicine. 'Sorry if this news is not what you were expecting.'

'Oh'.

'Yes, a new opportunity has opened for me and I need to move fast. I can work out my notice if you need me, but obviously the sooner the better.'

'OK. Well I am surprised Faye. Good luck with your new venture. I'm happy to work out your notice now. If you like, take the remainder of your holiday entitlement to see you through to the end of this week. If you're absolutely sure on Friday, email me to make it official.'

I sense an upper-middle-class power woman smile grace my face as I get up to leave. I sense a sadness enter her eyes, and it only confirms this is the right thing to do. I have outposhed her. I feel like a millionaire from *Grand Designs*. I could be browbeating my stockbroker husband into buying expensive Antwerp glazing for some holistic eco-bulb project in my Somerset garden and then giving the Belgian installers a hard time in the rain. I walk straight out to the lift. Nobody remarks me. The space I have occupied for over five years will be filled by someone equally forgettable. I bet nobody will even bother to inquire about my reasons for quitting. I won't tell them I've been moonlighting as a sleuth catfisher Skype sex impresario. I never got recognition. The only time I got praised was when I was the first to notice the fridge was leaking. Then the standoff returned when I forgot about a Greek yoghurt which lay camouflaged at the back. A post-it note in annoyingly neutral capitals (probably Aparajita's) appeared saying PLEASE REMOVE FOOD THAT'S GONE OFF.

I walk out of the office and feel dizzy again. I take the wrong lift because it looks empty. But in the corner there's a sweaty middle-aged man with a brow furrowed by career frustration who summons the next floor. But this time I don't get out. As the lift goes higher it seems to slow down and I detect a clicking sound under the hum of the floor. I clench my fists and take it all the way to the top. I walk up the fire escape stairs out onto the roof. The side railings greet me as I lean into the wind. The shrunken dotted world of people and vehicles below moves long without noticing me up here. I am invisible. And that's how I like it. The pocket-sized New York townscape of Croydon makes me wonder if my fake profile self will chat to faceless Marco again. The clammy anxiety I've been getting all week dries in a gentle breeze.

CATFISH HONEYTRAP

Maybe I need a break. I could go and visit my mum for a couple of days. But she could never be much arsed with visitors. As long as I reassure her that my frequent radio silence is due to work or parties rather than getting stabbed in an underpass, she's fine.

My wasted decade pales against the thrill of making my thousands now. I have discovered a second type of life, a type that occupies several made-up lives at once. It is running parallel to my disintegrating relationships, to the cold shoulder from Fiona, to unseen emails about cheaper energy tariffs, to the unopened local election envelopes.

I text Fiona 'today was my last day at work.' For once she responds straight away, like old times. *OMG have you been fired?*

I bite my lip. A real friend would call to ask if I went or was pushed. What a condescending bitch she really is. Anybody would think she never used to shoplift when at uni, including from the shop she lived above, and for no good reason. My money now is hard earned. Unlike her I don't have a knack of how to spend it since I've been working in invisible jobs for invisible pay for my adult life. I start a text explaining that I resigned, and by the way my bank balance is approaching six figures. But I stop myself. Dignified silence will test her better.

Time to treat myself. When I get home the handsome Marco Prendergast is online. My opening gambit is golden, cheeky, flattering and playful rolled into one: 'Player'

'*I've got respect for women and I'm no player*'

That's good. I'm fake and he doesn't mind.

'not the same if you're a guy though. You had my attention for hours last time and I was laying in bed in my underwear'.

'*I don't sext women but if u want to start doing that with me I would love that*'

'Sure Marco. Arun's into watching my face as I pleasure myself'.

'*Well can't we do it together with no one watching us but me xx?*'

I leave that on Seen. I don't have an answer to that reasonable request, not after all the bullshit I've been spewing.

'*Why were u hanging then babe? When are u free soon we can Skype each other xx?*'

He's sounding insistent. So much back and forth with an interesting man who boils down to the same thing. No-strings cyber sex.

Do u do u want to send u more of me but u got to do the same xx

'I did show you stuff'.

U didn't send me nothing tho really so I think u should now u sexy minx

I dig out some chubby catfish pics. There's one of a woman on all fours showing off her butt that he hasn't got from me yet.

That's not u your body don't look like that don't lie. Send me a pic of you in your underwear what u look like now cos all yours pics look different.

'It's me. I'm getting on my back now'

Not 1st one ain't. Do full body naked.

'I can't babe. My guy in New York is Skyping me face again. Want to finish me off?' I've been writing this same line to so many men over the months that it is worthy of its own predictive text.

That ain't u tho. Your a cat fish btw your being investigated. I don't mind a fake profile. But I want real pics of you. Your not the person u said.

Oh fuck. Is he for real?

'He's back. Did my flash work?' That was a good save. I stare at the 'Sent' sign. Staring 19:16. Staring 19:17. Staring 19:18. Still no 'Seen'.

Fuck.

Too late. Marco is offline.

*****

I have made a rule for myself. No emotional attachment. No shitting where I eat. Marco is just some stranger across the Atlantic. I'm experienced enough now to know that investigating a catfish means nothing at all. Besides, Eminem has replied. My hand trembles as I click on the pics he's attached to his message. I familiarise myself with my relax mode. I type a 'hey sexy.' He takes a few seconds to see my message.

Then the typing dots drag before a recording appears.

His voice whispers 'you're interrupting'.

Then a couple of grainy pics appear. There's a woman is sleeping in his bed. What sort of arsehole takes pics of his partner when she's asleep? Even I wouldn't do that, if I had someone to share my bed. I scrub my eyes with the cuticle of my thumb. Then shamelessly I think of saving the pics for a future sex chat. I don't bother when I realise there's no logistical way of explaining a pic taken by someone else.

What have you been up to Faye?

Creative stuff, I reply. It's not a lie. But I'm not writing the novels and screenplays I've been letting on. He doesn't send any more pics. The dots turn into text.

Sounds like uv gt it all planned out

'what about you MnM?'. It seems weird spelling out his assumed name, even if he looks like him in real life. I scroll down to see a pic of him and a group of others in dark suits. 'Just looked at your FB page. Sorry if there was a funeral'

Yh it was my grandad he was like my dad miss him man. It's Asher btw.

'Asher? Your name?'

Mhmm.

'So what's your story, Asher?'

R u ready for this one lol

I say yes, searching in vain for a popcorn emoji.

Well I went to jail for six years I gt out a couple years ago. Now I'm setting up my own ground works company, and do ground works.

'oh wow ok'. Something about ground works makes me giggle. Months of predictable online chat are a poor guide for Asher. And he was a criminal. I'm proud of my ability to interpret the *welcome back* messages on his profile. Less proud of my mindset when I google Bonnie and Clyde and find the phenomenon known as hybristophilia.

I'm behaving now days n just try to live life

Yes, behaving as in messaging me with his girlfriend sleeping next to him. I'm googling 'Asher' and scrolling for convictions. There's a press report from Essex about an Asher Cole being sent down for manslaughter. There's a grainy photo that looks like a younger shavenheaded version of my muse.

'so obviously you survived prison'

He's not replying. Maybe the woman has woken up. No. The dots are back.

U know wt Yh it gets bad but it is wt it is I wouldn't change it for nothing I met some of my best friends in there that would die for me

'wow I would never have thought of that. Friends from the inside'.

When I'm in a bad place out here I just think we're I've been and how I can can do anything in life

'yeah it's fascinating', I reply. It actually is. I'm pretty sure I would have read about him or detected some sort of restraining order. I don't feel unsafe for myself. Besides, my morality sensors vanished months ago. I'm getting a kick from getting his life-story while his lover is dozing next to him. 'Never really thought about life like that'.

That's right babe.

'I went on a disastrous date with someone who wouldn't shut up about *Prison Break*. No idea if that show was realistic'.

I watched that it was a good one

'Yeah, the main actor was fit lol'

Eminem-Asher replies with a gracious thumbs-up.

But see u watch it on tv. But it's much worse.

'Yes, I suppose'.

But u always have a good times in there make the best of a bad situation. I spent 2 years in Category A, then six months down south called Ford. D cat.

CATFISH HONEYTRAP

Categories A and D jostle in my head. One sounds extreme and the other mild. I'm not going to pry.

So D cat gave me a chance to get out into town and try to sort myself out for release. Had some fun too.

He sends me a video of him bare-chested surfing on his belly down a rinsed corridor. He's got a tattoo on his upper back that I'm seeing for the first time. How do they even get smartphones on the inside? I'm not sure what I imagined the inside of a prison to look like. But I'm sure it would have been more like Alcatraz than this non-descript concrete interior that could pass as a high school or sports centre.

This shit that goes on when inmates get bored lol.

'I've never chatted to anyone like you before'. My message remains on 'Seen' beyond the five-second comfort range. 'Someone who's been inside I mean'

lol where I come from me n all my friends have been locked up. It's just normal lol if u no wt I mean. I first got locked up when I was 15.

My hand drifts to the inside of my thigh and I stroke it slightly. I wanted Marco. He's my online good guy to balance out my ex-con. I check his account and will his 'Last Seen Online' status to morph into 'Online', and dots of tremulous typing. But he is ghosting me. I switch back to Asher. I listen to his voicenote.

'So when are we going on a date babe?'. An optimistic voicenote. Outrageous, too, with a mysterious woman asleep next to him.

I stall him with a question.

'So you let your hair grow back then?'

Mmhmm.

'So you don't look like Eminem any more then?'

Lol what? x. Oh yeah, MnM. What about our date?

'Got another question before I can answer yours'.

My messages stays 'Seen'. He's obviously waiting patiently. I play his prison video again. When he stood up after sliding down the corridor there was a pentangle tattoo on his upper back.

'What does that tattoo mean?'
Which one? The one on my back?
'Yeah, the Satan-worship one.'
Lol. It's the Sigil of Baphomet. Not Satan. But it means nothing anyone can do or say will ever hurt me.

I reply with a devil emoji and a kiss, then go for a shower. Lukewarm instead of hot. The sexual encounter I'm not having with Asher is the one most vivid in my imagination.

*****

I dry my hair and think about a glass of Chardonnay. But I see there's an email in the Parsnip inbox from Elaine. She's a punctilious ballbreaker and I'm going to need every ounce of sobriety to close her file. I answer her email: *Hi Elaine. I'm sorry it's bad news. Did my colleague in Kent send you the proof?* I'm sounding like the doctor giving the diagnosis again, or like Sarah Lund from *The Killing*. I never get the tone right in text. Luckily she replies straight away, asking to speak on the phone.

'Hello, is now good to talk?,' she says with a stilted tone. There's an image in my brain of Hyacinth Bucket cocking her head on a landline receiver, bovine and blank-eyed in consternation.

'Of course, Elaine'.

She is purring with thanks for all the print-outs of the Messenger chats, the emails, the photo I took of him at the hotel reception in Tunbridge Wells which I booked under his name and date-matched with the messaging between Imogen and her husband. The pics of the sexmessed room, complete with half-empty bottle of Bushmills by the bedside that Elaine would spot as his favourite. Everything worked well until actually made to leave the room. I freaked out when an elderly cleaner was directly outside my door with a binbag open-flapped in a triangle. The poor woman was startled in a benevolent way, as if she was witnessing a manic episode unfold on the fourth floor. As I sat at reception waiting to confirm the checkout I half-expected the

5ft-tall South Asian woman to come and see that I was ok. Those five minutes waiting for someone to appear raised drops of sweat on my neck. I lifted my gaze to the ceiling. The criss-crossed striplights made me dizzy.

It was a pricey job. It never occurred to her six-figure earning husband that asking me/Imogen to book the hotel with only two days' notice meant paying over the odds. And it was a rip-off. Worn congealed carpets and frosted glass above the room doors and claustrophobic drab throughout. But it was a tidy job and his Bedfordshire battleaxe is paying me back.

'What happened? How did you discover them?' Elaine is sounding like a homicide detective. I feel as if I'm supposed to say *heart attack, sorry*.

We found his fleshy bulk on the toilet at the Travelodge.

'Sorry for the gory details Elaine, and please appreciate the need for confidentiality. Basically that hotel chain uses contract cleaners. The Parsnip colleague in the West Kent area does agency work and we got her to take the shift when Roger and this Imogen woman were staying the night.'

I'm a freaking genius. Nobody living in a five-bedroom detached house in Woburn, a village with an actual abbey next to it, is going to have the faintest bullshit radar for the lives of the cleaning underclass.

'OK'. She lets out a sigh. There's the slightest clink sound of something being swallowed. Maybe she has a drinking habit like her husband.

'I'm so sorry Elaine. I'm afraid we deal with lots of cases like yours and it never gets any easier'.

There's a silence on her end that stretches a couple of seconds beyond the normal comfort zone.

'I bet you make enough money out of it though'.

Oh. It's like that, is it? If only everything about my relationship with Elaine ever since Summer sent me the guest list hadn't been complete lies and fabrication on my part, I would feel offended. If this were a real cheating case, I would advise her to save her frustration for her tubby husband, not the messenger.

'Well, we perform a professional job Elaine'.

'Hmm'. There's another ice cube clink sound. She's probably necking gin and tonic. She sounds the type.

'We're also cheaper than the competition. They're too much stuck in the pre-digital age'. I'm proud of parrotting Brian's wise words. Boomer words to silence her insinuations.

More silence. I hear her breathe out.

'Anyway, Elaine. We received the thousand-pound downpayment. With expenses included, the remaining bill comes to three thousand'. She can't see but my eyes are wide open in greed.

'The money's not an issue, Faye'.

What? I need a couple of seconds to digest what I've just heard. I've been Fiona's Parsnip contact 'Jacqueline' in every dealing so far. There's no way she could gave guessed my real name.

'It is Faye, isn't it?'

I press my lazy hand through my hair. How did she know? The Parsnip website reveals nothing about me and the landline is always set to unidentified caller.

'Faye, I did some investigation of my own. You were friends with Summer. Roger and I came down to uni twice and you were housemates with our Aggie'.

Oh. Fuck. Is this it? I'm finally rumbled. I suppose I could tell her that visit came a few hours after her beloved daughter had spent the morning scrubbing her one-night-stand's vomit out of her carpet. But I'll keep that in reserve.

'Anyway, this isn't the first time Roger's been behaving like this. I'm divorcing him now. I'm just surprised to see someone like you involved in such a sordid business as this'.

'Elaine, it's not a nice line of work all the time. But we get results. And I'm sorry he's been acting up'. The ball is back in my court. Her husband is innocent. But in reality he's guilty. Like all men.

'Well I'm transferring the payment now. Just one more thing. Summer's wedding is coming up at that castle in Sussex'.

'Yeah?'

'Well, Roger and I are invited. I'm not sure what stage our lives will be at that point. And I don't want to embarrass Aggie or Summer. Aggie's been through a lot'.

'OK'.

'I'm not looking forward to going through another social event pretending everything's normal between me and my husband. But it's for Aggie, too'.

'OK'. What is she trying to say? She can't confide in me after just pulling all her superior bullshit.

'Well, I would really like to know if you're going to be there. There are going to be loads of people but I'm not sure if I can face being reminded of Roger's infidelity'.

Blimey. Hyacinth is really pushing it. It wasn't me who had a fling with her husband. It was my imaginary Imogen frustrating her horny husband with a no-show. Then my imaginary cleaner provided fake evidence. Elaine's lucky that I've got a total of eleven catfish cases simmering away from Summer's wedding list, and I'm about as likely to attend the scene of my crime as I am to run one of Fiona's halfmarathons.

'It's OK Elaine. I can't make the wedding anyway. You go and enjoy yourselves. I hope the divorce goes as well as can he hoped'.

I only absorb the call after I end it. Sometimes in my work there are moments when a sudden wind blows through my chat. But it's normally a recrimination for being fake or a threat from a girlfriend. I've never had someone I vaguely know in real life try to make me feel bad. Apart from Fiona. And Fiona will turn into Hyacinth in twenty years.

*****

I decide to go out. I need a dose of the real world. I should get my lazy arse to the gym. All these months of catfishing and I haven't been on an actual date since the *Prison Break* pisshead. I could make a point of making prolonged eye contact with one of the men there. It's no good. I'm not the metropolitan girl of chance dates in gyms. I'm a reclusive faker torn between mystery man Marco and Asher. I straighten my hair and fringe, and apply eye-liner and lipstick. I wear boots, despite the warm evening. I reckon I'm going to be on my feet for hours, and I don't want to give myself any excuse to bottle my courage and take a cab home.

I meet Asher in a neutral space. It suits my confused mind, which is not sure whether this is still a PI opportunity to take live pics of my most successful male catfish. I'm not making the mistake I did with that tosser Tim the other day who spent half an hour taking about all women being bitches before he actually followed me halfway down the street after I made it clear I was going home alone. Then his tosser girlfriend blocked me without paying anyway. This time I've found a Costa coffee in a busy place with three exits. Asher's gaze is intense, direct. After his stubbly face brushes my left cheek in his kiss we sit down to chat. His eyes won't leave me. After I showed him the catfish profile I pretend a stranger has made of him a kind of bond has grown between us. I know better than anyone his surprise. I'm initiating myself into his world with one foot keeping the exit ajar behind me.

'I'm not surprised', he says without breaking his stare at me. 'We used to get phones smuggled inside. Tons of women got their kicks messaging us'.

'Oh yeah?'

'Yeah, loads of them catfished other women's pics. Or sent us photos from ten years back. Married women too'.

I feel myself blushing as I sip my coffee. I love how he can still surprise me after knowing what I know. I can't believe I just showed him naked evidence of my catfishing and he batted it away stoically.

'Wow, anyway, funny to think this is the first time we meet in person'.

Looking back at his stare I can't work out how old he is, probably late twenties. There's a trace of a tattoo looking like a bruise disappearing down his neck. For a moment I imagine the mystery woman leaving a hickey on the other side to match his tattoo.

'Look, sorry this is short darling. I've got to meet my probation officer. Are you free for a drink tonight?'

I feel like he's just screened me. He wanted to make sure I was real, that I would show up. And he assumed I would just say 'yes' to meeting up tonight. The self-confident fucker.

—————————————————————

Asher's picked a new Latin American bar in Elephant and Castle. I arrive fifteen minutes late, a premeditated ploy to turn the tables on him and repay the tension in kind. But it's difficult because I'm dying to see him. When I arrive he's sitting at a corner table by himself, manspreading the space for three and taking sips from his Corona. He's busy scrolling on his phone and doesn't notice me walking in.

'Hola'. My Spanish icebreaker falls flat.

'Oh, hi darling'. He plonks his phone down as he stands up to kiss me on the cheek.

'Sorry I'm late'. The bristle from earlier has gone. He's shaved and smells good. His kiss still gives me a tingle.

'No worries, darling. And, wow, you look amazing'.

'Thanks'. I sit down. He puts his phone in his pocket. 'What were you looking at on your phone?'

'Ah nothing darling. Stay here, I'll get you a drink'.

He's lying. But so am I. I swivel my seat round to watch him standing at the bar. He's got muscly things and a peachbutt. I'm going to ride this evening out to the obvious conclusion. While he's ordering I log into I-wen Chang for the last time today. There's a shitpost on her profile page. *You're a fake account.* It comes from a Facebook account set up today with the lame name Hayley Robbins. There's no profile pic, no words in the bio. The message was posted five minutes ago. Is Asher catfishing? Is he secretly angry at the catfish site I pretend to have found accidentally and repaying me the bullshit in kind? That would explain his cagey reaction just now. I delete the post and block the faker. Later I'll tighten I-wen's security details further. Asher is coming back with the drinks.

After an hour of chat I go to the women's toilet. I stretch my arms above my head in the mirror and roll up on the balls of my feet and back down. I pull out a miniature bottle of mouthwash to rinse out the accumulated smells of coffee and alcohol and swirl it in my mouth before spitting it in the sink. We go back to his place and I suppress the memory of the mystery woman who was laying in his bed last night.

Chapter 9

After my night at Asher's HMO I feel like I am masquerading as myself. No longer wasted in the dark. Now I am sober in broad daylight. Even the walk confirms I am my South London self. In the taxi last night I was too busy managing his tongue in my mouth to notice where he lived. Asher's flat is down one of those streets where all the bus stops are too far away from the station to make it worth taking one. Then once you start walking you wish you had got the bus after all. When I reach his place it deserves its 119 followed by 'b'. The suffix denotes that it's a shithole.

Part of me is pissed off to see his basement flat in the light of day. It's better than my bedsit and it's not fair that someone like him can end up with accommodation like this after his time inside. I run my fingers over the wooden mantelpiece. I'm surprised to find it without dust. *I'm moving next week* he told me, as if anticipating my disapproval. I knock on his bedroom door and wait. Eventually, after a fucking minute, making me wonder if I-wen's there, he opens and leads me down to the spacious shared living room. He manspreads on the sofa and picks up his half-finished joint. There's a soapy damp smell, like washing being dried in a room without windows. I refuse his offer of a joint. Then he suggests a line of coke. I tried cocaine with Fiona once. It felt like swallowing two paracetamols without water for the payoff of slight happiness and sweaty cheeks. It's another 'no'. I'm a square after all, despite what we've done.

'Only kidding darling. I don't do any of that any more. I'm rolling this joint for my housemate'.

I smile. I'm relieved that another person in this house gives me a reason not to stick around.

'Look at you, plonked on the sofa. Why do you always keep everything at arms' length?'

'whatcha mean?'

'Well, water, coffee mug, phone, magazine. Why do you keep everything you want neatly around you?'

'It's my old prison routine darling,' he exhales and his eye light up. 'I also sleep in on Sundays'.

'Oh, did I wake you?'

He stands up in a flash and wraps his muscly arms around my waist. This kiss is slow and long. He tastes of toothpaste. He stares at me with a cute glint of surprise. His clothes looks strange, as if they're new. They're plain clothes, jeans and T-shirt. Plain, but definitely new. Then he unloads his remaining doubts about me. Apparently he didn't think I was real thing. His mate thought I was the catfish, and that he got my lovebite on his neck from some freak wanking accident. Fair enough. I am a catfish, just not *the* catfish or whichever mystery man/woman linked him up with I-wen. Anyway, I'm off the clock. And he doesn't need to know I'm ten times more focused than he thinks. I am a real, unpixellated version of myself.

'I know you're a faker', he says. There's a sudden chill in his tone.

I'm lucky to receive this broadside with my back turned to him. I concentrate on the zip of my handbag as if it's stuck, thinking about whether the lipstick inside coud be turned into a defensive weapon. I feel dizzy as the five seconds of back-facing silence wrenches a reply from me.

'What do you mean?.' The palms of my hands are clammy as I turn to face him.

His blue eyes do not break their stare. I'm trying to understand what I'm missing, about why there's a sudden escalation to confrontation.

But I detect a smile behind his eyes.

'Faker, yeah. I need a faker'.

His pupils seem to dilate into sincerity. I prop my right hand on my waist teapot-style. I'm bracing myself for something.

'I may have to go jail like six weeks'.

CATFISH HONEYTRAP

I keep my poker-face. I hate how I'm feeling a thrill from this. Asher is transgressing openly. My transgressing has been all covert.

'It's only a minor'. He looks like he's bargaining. I don't doubt his sincerity.

'My support worker says a character reference might help. I need to provide one and then I'm handing myself in'.

He reaches beside him, next to steel-framed coffee table, and pulls out a newspaper. He unfolds it and flips out a stapled four-page A4 document. It says *Simpson, Mathers and Singh Lawyers: guide to writing a character reference*. OK. So he's asking me for a character reference. Goody-two-shoes me sleeps with a bit of rough and then restores him to society. Out of all my dozens of catfish and sockpuppets over the past months, it's come down to this. I'm a faker faking sincerity for a man who is flesh and blood in front of me. And he had the gall to check whether I took illegal substances. The guidelines are a parody of Parsnip Investigations, asking me for my age, background, interests and, best of all, whether I perform charity work. In good conscience I am counting my 30% delinquency rate on outstanding payments as a form of charity for women whose boyfriends and husbands were going to cheat anyway.

I would have preferred to type it on the screen but I don't want to reveal my real email. Also in the list of *do's and don't's* was a rejoinder in bold: **Keep it brief. Magistrates are busy people and are unlikely to read more than one page.** I sit down and write out a paragraph in rounded girlie style, blushing on the inside at my juvenile script. He's staring at me. He must be thinking why I'm spending so much time with him instead of friends. The truth is I don't really have any friends. Apart from Fiona. And she's been doing Pilates, flying to New York, working late, anything really to avoid spending time with me. The palm of my writing hand is getting clammy as I finish writing.

'I'm going now'. I don't like the sound of my voice. I'm staring at him, trying to gauge the intention behind his blue-eyed stare. He's being intense and benevolent at the same time.

'Drive you home?'

'No thanks.' I don't want him to know where I live.

Asher winks and tilts his face back to the football on his plasma TV. I stand OK, but I can feel myself shaking. My heart starts beating fast as the sweat rises on my back. If this were work I would hide in the toilet. But here I can only trust the front door and the street outside. Whatever is happening between me and my new lover I can't make sense of it here.

*****

I get home and realise I'd left my room window wide open. The din of traffic has spread its own humidity and smell across my sofa. I switch on the light and mean to go straight to close the sash window. I know moths and spiders get into my room and should have closed before the light. It's too late. A moth flaps straight through the window and seems to make for me before the usual bulb. I used to cover moths and spiders with glasses and perform limbo stretches to get paper or coasters to back them into the bottom where I could shake them out onto the street below. Then I used hairspray which would make them go stiff and shatter on the floor. This time I squash it with a book against the wall. I scrape its entrails into the look and wet wipe the cover. I sit down to check on my sockpuppets, out of fucks to give.

My DMs have blown up. I've expected this day, of course. I could just never predict when. And I would never have guessed nice-looking Iwen would get this online walloping. She is too good, too, too wellbehaved.

'*Mate, you're full of shit. Are you supposed to be some Japanese stereotype?*'. That DM comes from a fake account. A Facebook set up yesterday with intials for a name and 5 posing pics all uploaded at the same time. Amateur. Fake accounts are a dime a dozen nowadays. Why do they think I'm Japanese? The racist abuse confirms this. 'Whale-killer' is a new one on me. I suddenly think of myself back at school, walking past groups of girls to sit on my own. They would slag me off to my face.

But these are fake accounts, trolls, cowards.

'I've got software that can see through your cam Fran. I'll show the whole family. Why the fuck are you doing this to me?' Ouch. I don't even remember the details of that guy. *Claire wth! Did you tell Alessia about us? She checked my phone and now she's fucking chucked me out. And I've got these bags of shopping. Fuck it. I'll leave it here.* Damn. I was overworking. Always block and delete after payment is made.

I breathe out slowly. I scroll through Facebook chats and spot several shitposts about I-wen. *None of this is the real world*, I say to myself very slowly, as if needing to convince myself. I wish I could confide in someone. I can't tell Mike without exposing the whole scam and hurting him. His last message was cringe anyway: *I was raised by two mums so I know how to respect women.* And I'm barely speaking to Fiona at the moment.

I'm impressed how I can take this abuse on the chin. And now I'm wiser. The whale-killer one has messaged four sockpuppets besides Jos. I block her on all. I don't feel guilty. Even though I am making it all up, I am tapping into something real. Men who try to cheat with me will have done it for real. Or they are going to do it for real. They need to be held accountable. All I'm doing is helping women see this before it's too late. All those dick pics and hours of dreary chat deserve payment.

They deserve me.

Back to business. I log into the Thompson profile. Like clockwork there's a DM from Joe Schmitt, the balding family man from Orpington with the possibly Nazi grandfather. *How was the tagine? x*

That evening, Marco is back. His goodcop vibes are going to expel the shitposts from my mind. Flirting with him will help me put my feelings for Asher in context.

Don't you miss me?

This was an easy one. Disarming and generous after his hissy fit about catfishing. Of course I miss him. I get to see his six pack and chat without putting out anything in return. Maybe my part-thrill, partlearning curve for male catfishing, will keep me away from a man who might have me to thank for keeping out of jail.

Have you been drinking?

'Just a glass, cheeky git. Not all Brits are pissheads'.

Hey I love that though. Love me some British traditions.

He takes ages writing the next message. I take the time to check out the new likes and supportive comments posted on my IKEA lampshade pic and a chubby outfit pic I catfished from a month ago. The believers outnumber the shitposters five to one. I-wen is the gift that keeps catfishing.

I've been thinking about you.

'Yeah?'

All the fucking time.

'Marco, you're a star. Arun in New York has just got on Skype. I'm a bad girl'. Nuclear option. Full-on channelling of Fiona's online freakshow.

I can send you a pic if you like. I'm so fucking hard right now.

'Oh yeah. I saw you hearted my cleavage pic.'

Yeah baby. One button down. You're missing the other two.

'I'm wearing that blouse right now Marco', I lie. 'I'm not letting Arun see it'.

Could you take it off for me baby and show me?

'Don't be greedy Marco', I say triumphantly.

I'm thinking I'm playing too hard to get. There's not reply from Marco, not even a *Seen*. I unbutton my blouse and take a quick pic of my cleavage and upload it for him. The photo stays on *Sent*. I want his reply, or at least a *Seen*. That would be enough to strike a neutral pathway of erotica between us. I send a tongue emoji. I want to make it very clear that I'm in the moment. But he's away.

*****

The shitposts are back. I text Asher *what did you mean about faking? x*. It might be my last relevant chance to know if he really is going back inside. He calls me straight away.

'You ok babe?'

'Yeah I just want to know what you meant. You think I'm a faker?'

'Mmmhmm'.

I stutter a laugh. He's just outed me with a casual murmur, with the same ease as if he's stretching out his muscly arm above my pillow.

'Well? I'm all ears'. I don't like the tone of my voice. It sounds guilty and shrill, depressingly accurate rendering of my emotional state.

'Babe, I've spent years trying to be someone else, so it's cool'.

'W-what?'

'Yeah. I'm always being judged. Nobody has ever really known me'.

Now is the obvious moment to ask him. He's a man I've slept with who has a car and a sixth sense for fakeness. I don't know where the sudden insight came from. But I found a way to make him work for the next date. The FPIUK meeting is coming up and I need a lift and a plus one to this castle near Leeds.

'Asher, I'm happy to tell you more about what I do for a living. I think you more than anyone else will appreciate it'.

'Mmhmm. Well what is it darling?'

'Look. I've been invited to a meeting at a castle near Leeds next week.

I'm allowed a plus one for the lunch. I want that to be you'.

'Castle, Leeds, what?'

'Trust me. It's just a lift. In fact I'd rather you picked me up from the station at Leeds. Hard to explain but I need to travel alone but then have you there with me so you can sus the others out.'

There's a silence. Finally he speaks.

'OK Faye but tell me what it's about. This meeting.'

'It's a lunch organised by the Federation of Private Investigators of the UK. Not being funny but you're the ideal man to have at my side. If they're fakers, I need you to tell me.'

*****

Fiona's been quiet for a week now. Normally she texts daily. When she finally answers she agrees to meet in the Costa near my old workplace. It's packed out and she either doesn't or won't hear me say *Fiona* above the revving of voices. As I take my seat she seems distracted. Her phone is in her hand and she spends half her time glancing down and scrolling through texts. The atmosphere between us is so strange. She's holding something back, and she never does that. I want things to go back to normal, to when she joined me with the sockpuppets and laughed when I showed her how my ex fell for the Sandra one. But now it's awkward. She has a way of talking without communicating. The rainshower that caught her has robbed her of some of her dignity. Her hair is drenched and the dousing her face has exposes early wrinkles round her eyes, and a type of caustic forehead.

I confront her. 'Fiona', I sigh. 'I may not have a high-flying career like you. But I am successful. You won't believe how much I've made in the past week alone. But you wouldn't know, because you never ask. You're my oldest and best friend. And you have no idea what I've been doing.'

'Yeah, what *have* you been doing exactly?' She takes a step back, like I've just been threatening her in some way.

I watch her consider all the paths our conversation might go down. There's a moment passing between us that makes me unsure if she's about to frown in despair or smile in condescension. My heart is racing so much I can't even focus on her reply. All I get is the nasal tone, even worse than a Marketing boss, more like an HR boss, or the Libdem woman who was canvassing me that one time when I was leaving the flat and then dead-eyed me when she twigged she was on the wrong side of the road.

'Is this about taking another share? I offered you a grand for helping out with the Bradley case remember'.

Fiona snaps.

'It's not money Faye. Money suddenly seems everything to you, doesn't it?'

'Whatever', I reply. I should really have said something more mature.

But she had it coming.

'I know exactly what you've been doing, Faye. You need help. I'm not being rebarbative'.

Normally anyone saying a word like 'rebarbative' can just get fucked. But my heart drops as I can't think of any reply. Her face crumples as she grabs her coat and storms out. There's something extra about it. It's not just her usual vibe of being the most important person in the room. When she turns to face me before disappearing through the door, her look isn't smug. It's plain and almost modest, as if holding back tears.

It's as if I'm the one who's fucked up.

I exhale and go straight back home. The homeless man isn't opposite my stop. His absence symbolises the shift in my life. Fiona has some reason to avoid me. The hurt in her face embarrassed me into not wanting to pry. I'm about to cross my street but I stop and stare. My heart is in my throat. I-wen is walking down the street on my side of the road. She's wearing wintry jogpants and a bubble-coat. She is as clear as the fading November sunlight. She is no ghostlike image. She's a real-life human being. I hold my breath expecting her to walk past the steps leading to my communal front door. But she turns and goes up. I watch her punch in a code on the door. She pauses and does it again. This time the door opens. She goes inside and switches on the hallway light.

I stand frozen. Anybody noticing me would think there's something wrong, like a hernia or appendicitis. I stand behind a feeble tree bearing brown leaves and cup my hand on my stomach. I feel as if I'm about to have an out-of-body experience. I'm no longer an outsider, and no longer an insider. I have spent the best part of a year living through other people's eyes. Now it is being repaid fittingly by my prime creation. I am the catfish stalker getting stalked by my catfish victim. The hallway light starts to lighten the growing dusk and now Jos is leaving. She is not carrying anything. She walks quickly down the way she came. Now I am breathing, recovering my composure, and crossing the road. Images swarm my mind of threatening notes, bugging devices, and who knows what.

I'm so pissed off right now. My heart is faintly in my throat. I don't fear Jos. I saw her innocently in the bookshop, unbeknownst to her. There is nothing suspicious in my postbox, and no sign of forced entry or penetration of my bedsit. I bolt my door anyway and decide to channel my consternation towards my work. I go straight to the creepy 'Bumpy' profile who's been drip-feeding me his pathetic life of able-bodied benefits and a girlfriend who could do ten times better without him. I'm taking out my frustration on him. I suspect the Kerry woman will welch on the payment, but I pick up the old thread anyway.

The trail of chat seems to be that of a sex offender. Yet here I am, desensitised, rolling with his rhetorical punches. He says he'll pick me up, or send a cab if that's too forward. He promises to fuck me like an animal. He always focuses on himself, without sparing any thought for the women he complains about. I video-call him. I shouldn't be surprised to see such a vulnerable and sad man on the other end of the call. His bullshit profile of the fast car and shades. His mind seems short-circuited into permanent self-pity. He's always the victim, never the perpetrator. His camera angles shows a single bed against a wall with sheets balled up in a mess. His room probably stinks of faeces. Then it's back to what he's going to do to me. He's wasted, typing *it'll cost you*, and slipping between sex and money.

Bumpy. You sad little man. Let me project my self-loathing onto you.

All screens are on. 3 catfish in action. Opening Clara, no new messages. Loads for I-wen. A list of blue-circle DMs list down the MSN chat bar. She has five new friendship requests. 2 women and 3 men. I'll block the teenage-looking male and the other who looks elderly. I'll accept the thirty-year-old one, and both women. They're actual East Asian women twenty-somethings with surnames Zhou and Chen. They'll network I-wen's plausibility. Then a quick log in as Joanne to respond to Joe Schmitt's inevitable flirt and then a final look at takings and projections for this month. They're both healthily in the black. God I'm tired. Tired of I-wen, tired of men actually writing the things they write.

Fuck it. I need my own fun now. Time for Marco.

*****

Ur still not doing what I'm asking you.

I can't tell why he switches from normal prose to crappy grammar. It's like listening to Tony Blair using glottal stops. But as an opening chat line it's not a bad one. Persistent and assertive without being overly domineering.

'i cant distract him long enough', I reply unwittingly matching his poor grammar. 'sorry i'm no good at this game lol'.

In a min I'll prob block u as I'm not sure if you're real

'ok let s stop'. I'm experienced enough to know he's not going to do this. 'you're horny but i can t shake my bf'

Bf? I thought you said he was your fiancé?

'Yeah, fiancé. Sorry I say it without thinking'.
Just answer my Skype.
I stall him by answering with the cam wrapped in a red T-shirt. A blood-red shade projects back to me on the camera box.
I know you keep turning it off
'it is on', I lie. 'Sorry, cant hear you, or see you'
Turn your light on. So I know your real please
'1 min'. I end the call and give it a ten-second time-out. 'i cant. Sorry my fiance's back on my Skype call. I can't shake him again'.
Why do you keep doing that on purpose?
'I'm not'. Five seconds of 'Seen' ensues. There are not typing dots coming from him. 'its not an angry sex session is it? Lol'
Are you female?
I get a missed call. His next call I accept. It's his naked crotch and he's semi-hard.
'i see you. Wtf youre hot'. The T-shirt is still cloaking my cam.
Show me you
'cant see me right? its dark anyway'
No
I yield by panning the open cam down to my naked legs. 'Youre getting me wet now'.
Fuck. That's better. His swearing smacks of sincerity.
'Tell me what to touch. I want to touch what you tell me while my boyfriend Skypes my face'.
OK but I want to see you too.
My hand is between my thighs. I scroll through his karate kick pics. They're all taken from behind. No head. No face. Who is he really? 'You got me nasty now lol. Arun's jerking. I need to stay quiet while you tell me what to touch'.
I'm into this now. All my months faking these online encounters and now I'm finally doing it for myself. I should be sparing with the name 'Arun' in case he's more than just a Linkedin contact with Fiona's

fiancé and uses this for some sort of bragging later. But the name's slipped out before and Marco never made anything of it.

'Arun's jerking at my face. He doesn't know you're the man turning me on'.

Call me now. I need to see you.

'I can't baby. Arun's watching me. It's so cool you're letting him do this'.

How come he can see you and I can't?

'He's watching my face. He doesn't know I'm chatting to you. He thinks I'm chatting to friends'.

He seems like a total loser.

'Yeah he is baby. But it's all good because I'm focusing on you'.

Turn the light on and let me see you.

'I need to stay quiet. Arun's watching. But I'm loving this Marco'.

He calls me a again. When I accept, all I get is his eye up close. The cam is shaking slightly. It's hard to tell if it's from nervousness or wanking.

'I love your eyes. Keep going baby. Give me this pleasure so Aaron won't pester me for virtual sex again'.

Oh so he's Aaron now? What happened to Arun?

He drops the call. Now it's messaging only.

Show me you now!

'Sorry mistyped. Autocorrect lol. No, keep going baby. You're pleasing me and doing my fiancé a favour too'.

I get the typing dots. Nothing appears except an angry emoji. I reel off a stream of dirty talk. I'm a natural. And my pleasure is building as I scroll up to the shower pics he sent me from a few weeks ago.

Tell me about you.

I start describing my body. But then he wants to know about my professional life. I just say Marketing. There's no way he would believe me being a PI and being honest about catfishing would break our spell.

You know I've got an app that can unscramble your lens?

That's an odd thing to say. Is my red T-shirt some new level of kink that's escaped me. I stop thinking or replying as I climax.

'I just came baby'.

There are more typing dots. Three angry emojis, then a line of abuse.

You're an absolute joke.

He seems genuinely indignant.

I know everything.

There are more typing dots. But nothing comes, not even any angry emojis. If I've hurt him I need to appease.

'I've been selfish Marco. We should stop doing this'

More typing dots follow. All I get is a question mark.

'This is risky and part of me feels bad about Arun'.

Why?

'Well, this was always his fantasy. He even asks me to get random vegetables from the fridge and pretend they're sex toys'. That was egregious information to volunteer. But it's so cringey that there's no way Marco would know about it. Men don't talk about sex, even if Aaron is more than a Linkedin contact. And no man would confess to a vegetable fetish. An alien fetish is the absolute limit.

'So yeah, I don't now how much longer I can keep this secret'. I type this just to pass time. The silence from Marco is a bit antagonising.

But the dots return.

Why the fuck are you doing this to me?

I gulp. My heart sinks. I don't love this man but I have no desire to hurt him. I reply with a question mark.

ur an absolute joke fi!

Then he blocks me. I breathe out, deflated. I wonder what 'fi' is supposed to mean in the heroic new age of internet speak. I check the urban dictionary but it isn't much help. It would be weird if he meant 'fiesta'. 'Fifi' is apparently prison slang for an artificial vagina. Well, I suppose it's not beyond the bounds of possibility that a successful businessman obsessed with Japanese culture would not know about the parallel world of fake sex. But I'm not fake or artificial. Well, I always was with him. But my pleasure was real.

Chapter 10

When a guy I've catfished opens up to me, revealing his intimate secrets, I feel as if he's picked up a dinner bill I had planned on sharing. Now rather than feeling obliged to pay out on the next date, even if he's not actually expecting it, I find myself blurting out some personal information of my own. The worlds are blurred as much as the unwitting ceiling and flooring linking us. I've been in this bedsit three years. I assumed the psychotic night-time screamer of the first year and the rehoused vibrator/toothbrush woman afterwards would be the sum total of my neighbourhood drama. But now there's a twist. The last man I slept with is living in the bedsit above. No more angry-sounding toothbrush/vibrator now. That unhinged woman has been gone for weeks. But a stalker? Or someone being used by a stalker?

Where do you actually live darling?

His latest text is persistent without sounding creepy or threatening. I reply South London. This could be anywhere, Streatham, Plumstead, Tulse Hill, or the shitty bedsit I inhabit five metres under him.

'Near Croydon. But don't worry Asher. I just need the lift from Leeds station. I'm visiting folks up there'.

Pick you up and take you to King's Cross then?

'Honestly, Asher, I'm fine x'.

The to-and-fro of people along my road indicts my mis-spent months of online encounters. Two men part ways as I cut through them on the pavement. One is wearing a hoodie, and seems a late teenager if his open-faced companion is anything to go by. The hooded one whistles, bizarrely, as I walk past, and his short-haired friend nods appreciatively, mumbling something that falls out of my earshot but which does not sound like endorsing a wolf-whistle. As I mount the steps and check that they are not following, it occurs to me that they could be serenading my stranger lover upstairs.

CATFISH HONEYTRAP

Now my other world is colliding with my shrunken self. I haven't gone mad. It is a reality. Asher has moved in upstairs. The borough has a sense of humour. How the fuck did the council put him there? Maybe my character reference did it. It's smaller and shittier than his basement, but hardly a halfway house. His car is parked in an impossibly tight spot. The spoiler and red sticker line beneath it make the Golf GTI look like a criminal car to me. Not that I ever learnt to drive. Sometimes on leaving my flat I look up through the stairwell to see his door ajar. It seems a sign for something, maybe for the hoodie drug dealers from outside. I'm becoming an expert at tracing Asher's movements. Music being played means he is cooking, unless it's hiphop. Then he's shagging the mystery woman. When his television is faintly audible, he is not doing anything at all.

*****

Four hours later I'm waiting in a pub around the corner from Leeds Station. I've become a parody of myself. Over the past three weeks since I decided I was coming I've added a total of forty-eight men with Facebook profiles in Leeds. Eleven have been chatting and three cheatables have arranged to meet me at this pub in the hour between my arrival and Asher texting that he's ready to pick me up. Two men got hooked by Jos and one by Ellie. Fiona's not with me to pull off the crazy hair profile pic and Jos is Chinese. So I'm lurking two tables behind the bar, turning to the tried and tested tactic of the catfish standup.

In the event only the two Jos catches show up. Hilariously, Polish Igor and Yorkshireman Henry are chatting to each other as they order their drinks at the bar. What do two late-twenty-something men with girlfriends have to share? I would think fashion tips. Henry's wearing a flannell shirt that's too formal and Igor is braving a T-shirt in the cold. Anything to show off his biceps. If they were women they would own up to meeting a date. As men they should just come out with it. Both meeting a chubby Taiwanese social worker doing a tour of the north?

What are the chances?

Asher has texted so I need to finish the job. I take four pics of the men from behind and one four-second video. The next move is riskier. But I'll never visit this pub again anyway. I pretend to take a call from Asher and approach the bar. *Yeah I'm in the Head of Steam, near the station.* Three seconds of silence. *No it's called the Head of Steam. Hang on I'll take a pic for the bar.* As I raise my phone both Igor and Henry obligingly turn their heads to look. Both their faces get in the shot. *Yeah, got that pic I just sent? Cool on my way.*

After Asher parks in the visitors' section of Hazelworth Castle he holds my hand and guides us into walking a short-cut across wilder grass to a trimmed perfect square by the entrance. Even in the overcast November skies it looks vibrant, as if someone has carved a bowling green in the middle of nowhere. The weak late-autumn sun is peering occasionally through the wind-strewn clouds. The clods of grass are clumping under my shoes.

After signing us both in we mingle with about two dozen suits clasping either coffee or prosecco. Being greeted by Brian in the flesh gives me the momentary thrill of recognition. Close-up he looks like my father. His face seems swollen, with flesh pushing his skin to stretching point but with hints of youthful handsomeness twenty years underneath. It just occurred to me that I signed myself in as Faye Gardner. Nice work idiot. After about five minutes chatting and Asher being silent, my lover pulls me aside.

'OK darling I just need to do an errand. I've got some groundworks to do near here. I'l be to-ing and fro-ing for a few hours'.

Groundworks, what? I've been so busy *not focusing* on my handsome plus-one that I'm taken aback. How dare he multitask? That's a privilege reserved to me.

'OK, just text me when you're coming back OK?'

As he kisses my cheek I feel glad he's out of the picture. Asher was the only dangerous man here. These men in suits are about as suspect as the health and safety visitor at my old workplace. One of them hovers into view, timing his talk perfectly as Asher disappears around the corner.

'Nice to meet you', he says without introducing himself or asking my name. 'Word to the wise. Take this with a pinch of salt. Brian's trying to get us all credentialed. But don't fall for it. The real work is still being done by the little guy'.

I nod silently, counting the clichés and the passive-aggressive sexism. Luckily the prosecco flows at the hands of two uniformed servers. There are two other women mingling before Brian gives his speech. But another man gets to me before I can branch off in minority gender solidarity. The friendlier woman waves at me like a shy beauty pageant loser. But Brian is in my field of vision.

'What's the hardest thing about investigating infidelity then Faye?' There's a twinkle in Brian's eye. Either he's done his PI work about me or he had the resourcefulness to check the signing-in list. As I pause to think how to respond one of his colleagues farts a dollop of ketchup on top of his food, ruining the posh hotdog.

'Oh you understood my trade name', I reply ambiguously. 'Hardest thing, mmm. Well, the clients are a pain. Loads of times I get all the photo evidence and they start questioning it. You know, not believing it and withholding payment'.

Brian is staring with a frown. There's a cluelessness in his eyes as though I'm a crazy catwoman with five heads.

'Yeah, I bet. Listen, care to come and join the panel desk after my talk? We've been told about you, so it would be great if you could answer questions'.

One of the other two women is sitting at my side. She looks about fifty and gives me a matriarchal smile swallowed straight into a frown.

'We're just keeping the discussion to prepared questions', she tells me, in a tone sounding reproachful, as if I'm planning to go full millennial on them and scuttle away as soon as I get accreditation.

Thanks folks. It's good to meet up and to get a nice setting. We're doing well. Leaving Kettering conventions behind. Chuckles are accompanying Brian's speech.

First on the agenda before I open out the forum is the plan for accreditation. By 2015 our governing body wants us all to get licensed (...)

I sip some water and glance around obligingly at the sixty-or-so delegates sitting on the plush seats. It is actually sinking in. I am a private investigator. I'm an outlier, an oddball. I'm a woman under 40 in the company of centuries of solid experience. I will get an accreditation on my Parsnip site. Fully legit. I feel a warm glow of fuckyous to Fiona for ignoring me. I'm killing it.

Now the biggest challenge will be in road traffic investigations (...) criteria for training of new PIs will be sorted at the next annual meeting. Then all of us should be at Level 3, basically proving we can do the basics. (...)

There's another woman, at the edge of the audience, at the back, holding a glass of prosecco. It is her. I am seeing her. I am transported back to the flanking ambush at Waterstones in Croydon, and my nearpanic attack running to the bus stop. Jos is sitting there, flesh and blood. I pinch my thigh under the desk. I scrunch my eyes shut. A second later she is still there. She's dressed in a lilac blouse, tights and what looks like a wollen tartan skirt. She's got the slovenly look in her chair, looking non-plussed as she glances around the room and sips prosecco.

Good thing is the training will be cumulative. Six-month probation periods will be accompanied with monthly feedback. (...) Some of this will be helped by younger entrants in this field. I'm hoping to learn more about social media and search engine optimisation from our honoured guest, Faye Gardner.

Blood is building up in my chest, My head is starting to throb like the seizures I used to get when I was a teen. I turn to nod at Brian, silently willing him to delay any question to me. I glance back in Jos's direction. She's still there. For a moment she locks eyes on me. There's a polite, low-stakes smile in her eyes. There's no hint of malice or shock. She is a friendly Dalek, a cheerful Sphinx.

Now we know there are strong feelings, what with most of us not being members of the FPIUK and worries of a closed shop of licensing driving out the little man (...).

My heartbeat is high. *Calm down.* There must be some other explanation. Am I a racist for thinking East Asians look the same? She could be a random Yorkshire Hong Kong PI turning up late to the meeting. But it's *her*. It's not beyond the bounds of the possible that jos has a twin sister that escaped me and who is based in the north. But it's not probable. It's her. My spell is starting to break and I'm getting the tell-tale dry mouth. Mercifully the toilets are to my left. There will be a whole panel and sixty delegates between me and the woman to whom I owe everything.

'Excuse me I just need the loo', I whisper to the bitchy boomer at my left. I sneak out behind the panel, whispering a silent *sorry*. Twenty seconds later I'm sweating on the toilet. I text Asher asking him to pick me up. He's replied straight away. *OK darling, give me 30 ok? Just finishing my errand now x.*

I blanche my face with cold water and dry it with a hand-towel. There's no damage to my make-up. The toilet door opens and for a split second I freeze, expecting my muse to confront me. But it's the other woman who is not the boomer bitch. I exhale in a feeling of ecstasy. I have harmless company. The taboo of walking out on Brian's speech has been broken by another member of the female minority.

As I walk back to my panel seat I feel refreshed and calm. I am not moving my head as I walk. A purposeful, dignified stride takes me back to my pride of place. The talk's coming to an end. Brian wants me to talk. After overcoming that attack I feel as though I could talk for hours. Even better. I look in Jos's direction. She is gone. Whatever hallucination or coincidence that plagued me a few moments before is temporarily out of mind.

*****

Asher is dropping me at the hotel I booked for my overnight stay in Leeds. The freezing rain is hammering in gusts as we leave the castle. It seems to chase me down the slope as we reach the car park. I'm shuffling my rain-drenched butt uncomfortably on his passenger seat. As I see Asher turn the ignition with rapid dexterity and spot the empty crisp packet with what in the dark looks like oriental branding on the outside it dawns on me that I've not been his only passenger today.

Even the way he swerves confidently to avoid the spine-dislocating potholes on the private road suggests that he's been doing chauffer errands. I look back at the crisp packet but the insufficient headlighting in the winter gloom stops me from making it out.

'You hungry darling? Did you get a chance to eat in there?'. His voice sounds far away because of the noise of the insistent hammering on the roof of the rain.

There's a drive-thru McDonalds on the way to the hotel. I feel a rush of saliva, out of hunger or suppressed nerves, as Asher draws our Big Mac orders across the threshold of the storm.

'Let's eat them in the car on the way. They'll get drenched otherwise'.

His intiuition is spot on and I am suddenly ravenous. A King's Cross BLT this morning and two proseccos at the castle should have been enough to tide me over. But I'm anxious eating. My burger bite is too big for my mouth, filling me from tooth to tongue. The gloom and the noise from the rain on the windscreen stops Asher from looking at my gorging spectacle. My taste buds are alive to the fizzing mix of inferior meat, mustard, gherkin and ketchup in their fifty-calorie mouthfuls.

CATFISH HONEYTRAP

'Do me a favour darling. Shove my Big Mac in my mouth'.

In a marvelous act of solidarity Asher eats his burger like a pig. He makes an audible sound of ecstasy as the car fills with the scent of fast food. Then he turns to me and says *you're gorgeous* as we find a parking spot on Regent Street. There's at least fifty yards' walk to the hotel and my umbrella gets inverted as the gusts of wind have picked up.

'Asher, there is something I want to ask you'. My hair is drenched and I'm holding the useless umbrella in a gesture of interrogation as we're standing in my hotel room.

'OK. Nothing to do with that umbrella is it darling?'

His words brush over me as I'm thinking of the best way to say this. His benign blue eyes are staring in apprehension.

'Nothing about where you want to stick that umbrella? I spent two years as a pretty boy in prison, just saying'.

His smile is lost on me. How do I ask him if he thinks someone whose London Dungeon pic he liked is stalking me up and down the eastern side of England?

'Joke, darling. What is it?'

'Just, you left the castle early. Did you see anyone entering as you left?' The insipid nature of my question strikes me as soon as I've asked it.

'Anyone, well yeah. There must have been dozens coming and going.

The car park was over half full anyway.'

OK. This line of questioning isn't going anywhere. I'll email Brian about it when I get home tomorrow.

'You ok then?'

'Yeah it's nothing'. I watch him roll up the damp sleeves on his forearm, remembering how his arm stretched behind my seat when he reversed us out of the castle car park.

'Got somewhere to go now darling. You've got an early train tomorrow, right?'

'Yeah, early night for me'.

He kisses me on my cheek and his tingly stubble is back.

'I've got half an hour free now though'.

*****

When I wake the next morning I text Asher to say I'm getting a taxi back to Leeds station. I scroll through emails and find a kind one from Brian. *Sorry you had to leave early yesterday but let's keep in touch! I'll send you news of accreditation in due course.* I doze on the train home. Passing through my ancestral nowhere lands of the East Midlands I grin at the success that London has given me.

When I get back to my flat, I check my phone and chav bun Leonie is in my bitchface DMs.

I still want to know.

Fuck it. Marco's blocked me and I've got my hookup living upstairs. I'll give her some half-truths and then I'll ignore her.

'I got chatting to Marco because he's fit and he was persuading me to do sexting. The guy's really into Skype sex. Not my thing and I can't remember how we got onto the topic.

Did you do it?

'Yes but pretty sure it was a while ago'.

When was the last time you spoke to him? I'm asking because every picture he uploads you seem to like. So I'll ask you again. When was the last time you spoke to him?

'Probably about a week, can't honestly remember exactly. You're his partner then?'

I get the infamous dots. She's going to explode in tears or fury and I don't want either. She probably thinks I can't tell her personality but I can. She has a clipped and arrogant tone unworthy of her trashy appearance. Something about her is off.

'I wouldn't have done it if I had thought he was taken'.

I don't give two fucks if he was single then

CATFISH HONEYTRAP

'OK. Is he with you now?'

What the fuck does that have to do with you?

'If you're not seeing him, why is it any of your business?' I might as well take the moral high ground. I'm banging my keyboard as if I'm trying to win an argument. 'You don't know me'.

I'm his fucking fiancee that's fucking why. Show yourself to me now. You've got a webcam right?

Do I block her now? No, I'm serving her shit back to her. I'm holding her heart and brain in my hands. I let it rest a few seconds and scroll down my unseen DMs. The proportion of 'fuck-yous' and 'cunts' is advancing on my usual flirt emojis, 'hey babys', and supportive dickpics.

Right, back to this bitch.

'I don't think you're really with Marco. I think you're freaking out because you're a cheater. Looking for some shit to project on to him'

I've been with this man for ages, you fucking slag. Where do you get off stealing someone's man?

'I'm not a slag'.

Aren't you though?

'I don't even know who you are. Look, whoever you are, I can let you know if Marco contacts me'.

The dots return. She's a fucking vampire.

Why the hell would you do Skype sex with someone you don't even know?

It's pretty desperate.

'I told him I had a long-distance boyfriend. He was getting off on turning me on in secret while my boyfriend was Skyping me on a different screen'.

What the fuck! But you were in a relationship?

'Yeah'.

No you weren't!

151

What the hell? She thinks she knows me. She's got a genius-sized brain hidden under her stupid bun.

Just to let you know you're a sad loser. And there's no way in hell my guy would go near a slag like you in real life. You're going to get exposed all over Facebook. Enjoy.

This person is not contactable on Messenger.

She blocked me before I could block her. I stand and stare at my own reflection in the sash window with the curtains I had forgotten to draw against the early winter evening. I'm staring so aggressively that if I were on the ground floor anyone on the outside would think I've spotted them. The rain's falling in a constant drizzle, like the indistinct scenery of a late-night TV static screen. The half-bare tree boughs on Fiona's side of the road are pitted against a dark sky, both looking as grey as my bank balance. I should just go ahead and pull the curtains to. But I freeze, as if I'm a goldfish staring out of its bowl, or my grainy reflection is about to portend a revelation about the identity of my shitposting stalker.

I wish I had an exit strategy. Elaine gave me one with her *Don't come to the wedding!* I wish I had a magic wand to wish it all away. There is no way out. I am trapped in a cyber box. Anything more I post now will be seen as more lies. If I dare to dive back into the chat from Jos and Asher, then I will appear as having seen the posts. Much better to ignore them. If I see them, I either have to lie more or block them. Both would be evidence of guilt. I'll leave it on 'Delivered', like Schroedinger's cat, both indicting me and not. If I admit my fraud, then it's all over. And frumpy Jos or Asher might come looking for me. Which would not be hard thanks to the council's rehousing scheme. But I leave the flat so little now that the chances of him seeing me are minimal anyway.

Sometimes I think I just need to resign myself to this life. My life is now split through five dozen fake personalities, with frumpy I-wen at the pinnacle. I feel mobbed each time I open any one of my three laptops. It's worse coming and going from this flat. I remember the

CATFISH HONEYTRAP

buzz I used to get when I moved into this place, of having to walk under hostilelooking towerblocks, the borough regeneration copse that interfered with the CCTV, and the tracksuited gangland figures looking to raise reminders of outstanding payments being due. I was slumming it for a chance of metropolitan life after a youth of provincial middle-class boredom. The stoners who hung around the newsagents were positively comforting when compared to the silent alienation of the small-town Midlands. Now as I leave my flat the old edginess is displaced by nausea. The wide sky dotted with cirrus clouds threatens to engulf me. All this air and space exposes me. Anything could happen.

I need to bulk-buy at the Costcutter. On my walk there I get the feeling that someone is following me. I haven't seen anyone acting suspiciously. But catfishing has given me an extra sense that most people don't have, or else they one they don't usually need. The supermarket seems so busy now I'm at danger of fainting in the aisle. Independent chubby women like me are not supposed to faint. I'm no dainty china doll, despite my fake profiles. But my head starts to swim and I hurry along. I ignore the special offers and go straight for sustenance. The wine fits fine into my basket but the Dorset cereals won't sit on top. I manage to keep hold of all the boxes until the till. Rather than slipping through my arms onto the floor they make it onto the edge of the belt without the cashier or anyone else noticing me.

When I make it back to the flat I breathe out with a sigh I normally make after my first gulp of Chardonnay. Now I am back at home in my screenworld. Outside is dangerous. Outside can spring sudden socialisation on you, whether it's a postman brushing past exchanging pleasantries or small-talk at the shop. I'm done with real world socialising and disappointments. I like my three screens and I like my front door. But they're closed and password-protected for a reason.

As I sit down to switch on my main laptop, there's the sound of hiphop and female moaning upstairs. Asher's prowess is now making her scream. Any louder and I could record her for my catfish audio bank. After two minutes of moaning that might have been an hour, a twopronged thud vibrates in the ceiling above me. I jump, even though it's a moan quickly follows in a way that implies it's not a dead body or anything other than my new neighbour's climactic sexual antics.

'How are you sexy?' I let my message linger as the woman moves around upstairs with a muffled voice. Then there's a sound of at least two doors opening. The main entrance is open with sounds of someone shouting '*yah, blood*' and a laugh. Then an upstairs door, maybe Asher's. The commotion draws me to my spyhole. Two black guys are walking past and up. They're the ones in the top flat above Asher. I go back to check for a response from my lover. My message is seen but he hasn't replied. There's another noise from downstairs and something indistinct from above.

Something draws me back to my peephole. I hear the faintest sound of footsteps in the passageway. I peer through and my body chills as if a ghost has just walked through me. Jos is there, looming into view. She is stopped almost perfectly in frame outside my door. She pulls her handbag strap higher up her shoulder and rummages through the bag part. She digs around like someone moderately drunk, because her bag is not big enough to warrant such an effort. Then she freezes. My heart wants to explode out of my chest. She turns to face my door head-on. Her face bulges towards me in the panoramic view. She mutters something indecipherable. For a moment I get flashbacks to scenes from *The Ring* as my shaking hand reaches the chain lock on my door. She is actually there, no here. A three-inch wooden door and two feet of floorspace separate me from the woman to whom I rightfully owe £63,567 earnings.

Sweat beads are soaking the door where my is staying pressed under the security chain. My horror film re-enactment is suspended when I see Jos tut under her breath, flick her long hair round and continue her way downstairs. I exhale, close my eyes in relief, and go back to my desk.

CATFISH HONEYTRAP

Asher has replied.
What's up darling?
His casual text draws me back into the sane predictability of hook-up culture.
'Not much. Bored, You ?x'. My fingers are shaking.
Buzzing. When we meeting up again then?

*****

I'm leaving Asher's request hanging. I need at least a day to keep him at arm's length. I want him but need to pretend I don't to keep him keen. Time to do some honest work. Tagine Joe Schmitt is Active and in my DMs.
Would you meet me for real? You're my type x
'Haha you're married Joe. I saw her with you at that pub, remember?' *She's a lovely woman. Mother to my three kids. But she doesn't understand me.*
I sigh as the cliché fails to shock me. Fifty-year-old faithful mother of three gets repaid with an opportunistic quarter-Austrian cheater.
'Even us chatting Joe, it's really cheeky. What with my fiancé in New York'.
You're a lovely woman Jo, are you sure this Arun is the right one for you?
I reply with a 'shocked' emoji and locate his wife on Linkedin. Antoinette hasn't answered any of the three Facebook adds I've been trickling to her since the evening in Orpington. With all this chat it's time to go nuclear with a Parsnip Investigations request in her inbox.
'Aaw he's great. He's a cheeky bastard like you'.
I bet love. Make sure he's not chatting to other girls right x
'Haha he's too busy trying to be, how can I say it? Creative. Yeah, creative on Skype'.
Aha. Creative eh? Do tell. x

The next day the weak wintry sunlight filters through my sash window, summoning me to make a decision. My body aches to stay indoors. But I want to see Asher again and am not ready to do the hello neighbour reveal. The *Quotidienne* café on Fiona's side of the road is only five or ten minutes' walk away. The footbridge is going to be a killer. But pedestrians are visible on the other side of the dual carriageway, so I'll have a decent chance of crossing it alone. I wait to hear Asher leave his flat above, then peer through *The Ring* peephole to check it's him walking down the stairs. I give him ten minutes to clear our building.

Then I leave.

The homeless man sitting opposite my stop always surprises me. He is slouching but his responses remain lightning quick. A seagull the size of small dog swoops down to snatch some of his upturned crisps. He flaps his arm out from a slumping position before the bird gets the chance to land. When I reach the café it's not even half full. I walk past it twice without going in. Then I stand outside and pretend to look at my smartphone for about three minutes before finally summoning up the courage to go inside.

'Alright darling?'. His stubble has grown slightly. He smells good again.

'Yep. Not bad for a faker'.

'Haha, shut up. Go and sit in the corner babe, I'm going to get you the same coffee as last time'.

I'm glad he chose the corner seats. There aren't many people here but my heart was racing as I entered the café. Now when I'm seated my breathing turns to my bedsit rate and I stop feeling dizzy.

'Nice place this Faye. Funny it's close to where I've moved'.

I look down at my latte and stir the long spoon into the foam. Maybe I can get him evicted. Another character reference condemning him could do the trick. This and a random couple of complaints from random catfish about Mandarin screams from the third floor.

CATFISH HONEYTRAP

'Anyway Asher, how's the ground works going?'
'Ha well I had to sack someone the other day.'
'Oh, what for?'
Asher fingers his smartphone and scrolls down the screen. Then he hands me his phone face-up. He gestures me to hold it. A sign of confidence which I appreciate. There's a text exchange from his workmate claiming his wife's pregnancy was having complication and he had to rush her to hospital. Mentions of 'bleeding' and 'mate' and 'sorry I'm a massive fuck-up' glaze my eyes. Asher's response is as borderline grammatical as his messages with me: *Listen you haven't exactly given me much faith to rely on you turning seems like every time we give you a sub you don't turn up and its not what we're after. If you genuinely want to work be there for 7:30 tomorrow.*

'Yeah, it doesn't look easy, being a boss', I say as I hand his phone back to him. His blue eyes seem to smile at me.

'So, what else is there to running a grounds business Asher?'
'Well I'm helping the the brother of a mate who's still inside. He's just come out of rehab but there's a judge who's refusing to let him have his kid except once a fortnight.'

My head suddenly fills with an image of Asher wearing a *Fathers for Justice* cape and standing on a brick chimney in full view of media cameras. But Asher is not a dad. Or maybe he is. If he's down on his luck then he would probably want to keep any kids at arm's length in case they end up following their father's criminal ways. This is so weird.

The more I dare to think about him the harder it becomes to consider 'Asher' and 'manslaughter' in the same space.

'Oh, so that's the grounds business, is it?'
'Well, there is more'.
'What more?'
'Ha you really wanna know?'
'Mmhmm'.

'I'm doing different ground work. Sister of a mate inside. She got divorced but is getting stalked by her ex'.

'Oh, fuck'. I look back down at my coffee. Why would he tell me that unless it's real? Stalking is terrible. Even I, a champion cyberstalker, know this to be true.

'Yeah. Police and mental health have been useless. She went on holiday with her son and found her ex had moved in while they were away. Then she got late night texts from him saying *have you remembered to lock the door?*'

'Oh that's terrible. So what have you done to help?'. Do I really want to know the answer?

'I punched the twat and gave him a warning'.

'Oh'.

'I thought he would press charges. But I'm in the clear so far'.

'Don't do anything extreme Asher'. As if I'm in any position to advise on extremes. As I say that a woman sitting at a table at the other end of the café rolls her head back in laughter. Then she jolts forward slapping her thigh as her long hair flops over her coffee.

'Then he stalked her with fake online accounts, and started talking shit to her friends. Her poor kid keeps asking why he has to write his name different at school. He thinks it's an adventure, poor lad, a mystery why he's not allowed to see his dad'.

There's a heavy feeling in my throat. If I break my stare from his blue eyes I will start crying. I hope he's enough of gentleman to assume they're tears for his situation, not for my own wretched self.

'Anyway, the police have been fucking useless. They can't charge him for stalking, only for harassment and malicious communications'.

'Oh, crap. Asher, I'm sorry. Really'.

'No worries Faye. I'm investigating some stuff, all these fake accounts'.

'Good. That's great Asher'. My knuckles must be turning the white with how tight I'm gripping my coffee. My mind races through all

CATFISH HONEYTRAP

the five dozen female and half-a-dozen males sockpuppets I've created, calculating the probability that this stalking ex-husband fell into one of my random chats. In a city of nine million, if he's in London at all.

'Darling you can drop the act'.

'What!?' I blurt out this response without thinking. All this sex and sincerity has melted the guardrails I've become expert at erecting against men.

'Yeah. You've been keeping a big secret from me'.

Oh fuck.

'I know you live downstairs, Faye. Don't be freaked. The borough put me there. I honestly had no idea'.

I exhale with a nervous grin. He stretches his arm across the table and presses my hand tight.

*****

I walk home with Asher across the footbridge. He holds my hand and walks a few paces ahead the whole time, like I'm a traditional wife in Jos's oriental culture. I appreciate it, but not for the reasons he's assuming. When we reach my door we kiss for a decent half-minute before he gestures me inside. I push back harder to guide him upstairs to his flat.

He leads me inside and I make a gift of myself to him. He is prison clean, like in his own place. If I were occupying this flat it would be smelling stale and fuggy after a week. Physical intimacy a second time will make him complicit in what he thinks I know. I press his shoulders and sit on his lap. He looks genuinely gorgeous as his blond-haired and blue-eyed stare looks up to me. He pulls my top over my head and kisses my neck and breasts. I open my mouth a roll my eyes slightly as I focus on an unrecognizable poster on his wall. We stand back up and I pull down his jeans. He puts me on my back and his hips move against me. I breathe heavily on his neck as he enters me.

*****

Two orgasms in half an hour of sex makes me a good sexual citizen. He is standing over me, staring down intently. I sense he's giving me a chance for a *let's talk about us* conversation. But I'm not ready. I refuse his offer of food and drink. Instead I go home, downstairs. I'm avoiding any real communication now that I've implicated him in my tacit faking. I'm not ready to escalate the hookup to situationship level. I'm not ready to lay in bed for hours. I sigh and sit down to do a couple of hours work. The Imogen account got a 'hi' from a woman who added me only a week after I set up this account.

'Sorry do we know each other?.' I might as well gambit honestly. It could be innocent and there's no money in lesbian honeytraps.

I don't know. Did I add you?

'Oh I see we're mutual friends with Trey Ashworth?.'. I remember the young clean-looking guy I added at random. Too young, I realise now, to have stakes for relationship blackmail.

Ohhh... yes... Elder Ashworth is my Husband and is original Elder up here in Globe

'oh Trey looks young. Sorry I think we just got chatting ages ago.' Seen but no reply.

'guessing he's your son?'

No, who are you to him?

'nothing but I used to live in Globe years ago'. I lie without thinking.

I should be a politician. 'He appeared on my feed for some reason'.

He's a missionary for the latter-day Saints for Jesus Christ. Who are you to him?

'Yes he told me about the religious history'. It takes all sorts. 'Nice way to spend some time'.

Her dots in reply are taking awhile. That is not normally a good sign.

CATFISH HONEYTRAP

But yes, I did friend request you because I thought you were a sister in the Mormon church. I did not know that you have no idea who he is and that you live in a different country.

'oh ok. No, I'm agnostic'. I'm hedging. 'Finishing a degree over on this side of the pond'.

Seen. Silence. What does she want?

'So no religiousness in me sorry'

How old are you?

'24'. I'm pretty sure I set Imogen's birthdate in 1987.

OK, well just letting you know that he has a girlfriend so if you have any intentions to speaking to one of my favorite elders with anything other than intent to talk about Jesus Christ or the gospel, please delete him off of your phone

'oh it's nothing like that lol. I'm in a relationship anyway'

OK, have a blissful rest of the day

'You too! Shout out to Globe!', wherever the fuck that is.

Ty

As I check out more DMs I hear footsteps past my door going upstairs. I rush to the peephole and see Jos walking up to Asher's. She's wearing a short tartan skirt and wintry knee-high boots. The noises above, an hour after I shagged him, confirm it's her. Asher shouts *Jesus!* What an actual fuckery my six-figure lifestyle has become.

Chapter 11

I jolt my eyes open on the armrest of the kitchen sofa. I must have dozed more than a few minutes, because my mind is fresh with a dream about being in a prison. But it was full of tourists and I couldn't discern whether I was an inmate or a visitor. Kevin McCloud's voice was narrating the tour. As I rub my eyes the uneven sound of paper or leaves being moved registers in my brain. The rustling might have been a bird flapping in the ledge overhanging my window. But it came from the other direction. For such a small place my hallway was long. I'm not used to someone entering without me occupying the same space at the door. The sound of muffled footsteps which registered as I lay half-asleep were foreign to my home alone lifestyle.

From my bedroom, where I would have been sleeping if I hadn't gone out, and relaxed with my wine before passing out on my sofa, there is the sound of an intruder. Something metallic drops in a direction that can only be coming from my room. As I prop myself on one elbow I see a light dancing along the gap at the bottom of the door. It could only be a torchlight. I can't bring myself to comprehend what is happening. I hear my Parsnip book being rifled through. Why the hell would a burglar want that? Is it Jos's doing? Or is Asher? He's a criminal who knows where I live, who knows I'm a rich faker. He said he was investigating fake accounts. I'll check if my door has been forced or if Asher has copied my key somehow. More drawers are opened, followed by a sound of rustling. Or maybe bitchface is after something. I sort-of intruded in her flat back in the spring. Maybe the Canadian dildo bullshit hurt her for real and she can't let it go. Whichever visitor it is, she is going through my papers like I'm in an Agatha Christie plot. Isn't this supposed to be passé in our digital world?

I get up and tiptoe towards the hallway where I can press myself behind the alcove in the dark and keep the front door in easy reach. I think about making some forthright noises. I could switch on some lights and let some books or plates drop with a thud. But that would mean confronting bitchface. I would either have to go into my room or see her escape towards the front door. I could flush the toilet and let her flee. But that would be humiliating and terrifying if she kicked in the bathroom door. I take my phone out of my pocket. I have Fiona on speed-dial. I don't even think of continuing the snub. She could get here in ten minutes. I dial her number and press my other hand to my other ear in the dark. My ring tone sounds four times but there is no answer. Then I hear a thud from my room and footsteps. Bitchface, Jos, or whoever, rushes out and down my hallway. I bite my lip as I shrink into the darkness of the alcove like a craven idiot. The door creaks open onto the silent night and slams shut behind the intruder. The pace sounds so light I know it can't be Asher. Killers aren't burglars, I think to myself. My breathing returns to normal. After two minutes I decide not to bother Fiona. The door was opened with a key. I need to get the locks changed. I walk to my room and survey the upturned papers, photos and opened drawers.

The photos are all still there. The intruder seems to have wanted my hand-written notes. But as I see them strewn on the carpet I count them all there. I flick through the Post-Its at thetop of each A4 page of bio details printed out at my office. They're still there, labelled with name, age, sex, and key personality characteristics.

Then I get down on all fours to search beneath my bed. I shake out a few books and magazines. I feel embarrassed that the intruder has not radically trashed my messy room. The bulky wooden wardrobe was supposed to go once I moved in with Jon. An unhinged door should make me spend more on IKEA. I go to double-bolt my front door, before returning to scoop my dirty clothes from the chair and floor. There's an old pizza box with crusts that rattle like bones when I pick it up. Then I see that the intruder has shoved some papers behind the box. The first three client files have been mixed up. The number ordering is wrong.

I know I should call the police. But my mind can't even process what all that entails. Giving a statement about possible stolen private documents and then having some non-plussed copper poring over my mugshots like the pyscho I am will get me nowhere. I'm not going to call Fiona either. She'll ignore me or think I've made it all up. I have no energy to break through the ghosting I've been subjected to by her. Part of me wants to confront Asher. I could take pictures and show him his handiwork. Something he couldn't wheedle his way out of with that smile of his. I could blackmail him to stop. But he has a violent past and besides, how many laws I have probably broken? Instead I stuff the hand-written notes into my jeans pockets. I'll look at them later in case I can work out what Asher, his lover, or Hoi, or whoever it is, wants.

In the end I take the initiative. I write a hand-writtten note in capitals and poke it under his door. *£500 in cash if you promise not to burgle me again. Poke this emptied envelope back under this door if you agree.* The £500's a drop in the ocean for me now. I've got so good at sleuthing now that I've upped my fees to outrageous rates in the hopes that nobody will hire me. But then anyone who does hire me is willing to pay a fortune, so I almost never say no. Then the self-selecting corrupt and narcissistic clients degrade my faith in human nature and dull any principled sensors I have left. £500 is nothing. As I close my door behind me my heart beats faster, as if it's the only organ in my body. I press my fingers to my eyes and look at myself in the mirror. The wintry sunlight pillaring through the window casts me in a ridiculous light. I should never have poked that envelope under his door. How can I be cold and formal after sleeping with him twice? Nothing I do feels right.

That night I awake drenched in sweat. The dream ebbs immediately as I transition from slumber to consciousness. The three computer screens stare at me barely perceptible in the dark. I move my damp head and turn my gaze to Jon's old pillow. The grainy neon clock says 3 am.

CATFISH HONEYTRAP

I feel so drained of energy these days that I even feel threatened in my own flat. This agoraphobia has been limiting my ventures outside to Costcutter for almost a week. The infinite sky overhead exposes me, trapping me because I know I cannot escape. Last week I almost cracked when I walked past the Wetherspoon with the youths yelling and staggering out onto the pavement. At any moment I've been expecting one of my catfish fakes to confront me and demand money, or worse, an explanation. I curl myself in my quilt and let my three laptop screens stare blankly at me. In the parallel universe in my head I never quit my job. I never sought revenge on Jon, or got wind of bitchface. I plodded away at my 9-5 until some graphic designer wanted to wife me. The parallel world of being a normal human being hovers in my mind as I fall back asleep.

*****

The next day my DMs blow up again. What the fuck?
'*The yellow catfish strikes again!*'
'*Do you ever stop, crazy bitch?*'
'FUCK!,' I yell. Then I start typing furiously, all in caps.
I slam down the laptop. I want to bring up the noodles I had just eaten. It's the same dilemma. If I click on the message threads they will appear as Seen. Then I'm cornered. It's fight or flight. I can't admit my guilt. I can't protest my innocence either. When I open an innocuous-looking message it reads *You and Claire are the same person aren't you?* When I reply with a *what lol*, Louis replies straight away with a *You're not the person you say you are.* I exhale and open Mike's message on the bitchface profile. I could not bring myself to chat to him all week. Part of me dies inside when I read his words *it's funny how you said you wanted to meet me. I wish I could oblige but my anxiety is keeping me home.*

There's a gentle tap on my door. The soft sound evokes something paternalistic, like a mental health practitioner coming to section me. So much of the closed-door drama of the past week has happened in my flat, on my screens and in my head. There is a chance everything has been a psychotic episode. But as I check the peep-hole I see it's Asher. As I unbolt the new lock on the door I feel a slight increase in my heartrate and a tremor in my hand. Asher smiles as I open the door. He is wearing a shiny tracksuit and a cap pulled backwards Americanstyle on his head. As he kisses my cheek I feel a faint glisten of moisture around his lips. He's probably just come from the gym. Then he hands me back my £500.

'Call me if I can help with anything darling', he says. The he goes upstairs. I sit at my desk chewing the nail on my forefinger as I hear him shower. Then he's back downstairs, into his car, and he drives off.

I spend all day doing paperwork and ignoring the hateposts before I take up Asher on his offer. I call him directly. I'm done with all the uncertainty. I open my webcam to make it clear it's a video-call with nothing to hide. At first he opens his cam from a laying down position.

His blue eyes peer down suspiciously at me. Then he hangs up. I call again. I know I'm intruding into his personal space, but anyway. After a minute he replies. I tell him everything, well not absolutely everything. I could tell him to keep the banging noises to a minimum since I was here before him. But he gets everything else, my whole lifestory, my whole me new career of monetizing catfishing.

Asher lets out a laugh. It sounds different from the previous times he's been jovial with me. This time it sounds real. I laugh, too, taken aback by my sudden honesty, by saying aloud the first thing that came into my head to a man who killed somebody and who is definitely sleeping with my number 1 catfish.

'I meant it Faye. Whatever shit you're going through, let me help. Life is a funny thing. We only have a few good years in us. Don't waste them in fear or lies'.

I feel myself welling up.

'Get some sleep darling'. He ends the call.

CATFISH HONEYTRAP

I breathe out and feel my whole body loosen up. I hear myself sighing as he hangs up the call. A beep comes from down the corridor. I'd forgotten about the lasagna which will be burning away in my oven. I rush down and switch off the oven. I double-fold a teatowell to take the food out. The heat pierces through the towel for a second before I can dump the lasagna dish on my worktop. I shove my finger under my cold tap and rinse it. Then I swear and guffaw. I'm not sure whether I'm crying or laughing.

I've lost my appetite, so I lay down and think what to do next. He's obviously taken at the moment, so I'm not expecting a knock on my door. Then I log into the bitchface account. There's a DM from a new fake address. Emily Russell is a lame name even by troll standards. But the message isn't. *Next time I'll burn all your files.* Then the dots appear. *And your stupid pizza boxes you greedy bitch.*

I get out of bed for a attempt at piecing together the evidence. I yank out my folders from under my bed and empty their contents onto the floor. I grab a pen and a pad of Post-it notes, brushing aside the pile of receipts I need to file. Details on all the catfish targets since last summer are laid out in an arc like it's a board game or Ouija board. I swap them around, trying to find links and patterns. No links or patterns appear before my tired eyes. Elaine has been the only one to twig my real identity. But I didn't go to Summer's wedding at her request and I can't suspect any grudge on her part. Now what? I gather the notes together again and stuff them back into the folders.

In the meantime I'm going to sleep on the minor issue of this pathetic blackmail burglar. The rain is hammering on my sash window, hard like sleet. I have nights like these where crap just piles on top of crap. And I can neither sleep nor summon up the discipline to do some night-time catfishing. I message Asher: *you said you wanted to help. Can you come downstairs and spend the night with me please? x*

Two minutes later, the knock on my door sounds soft like before. I'm getting used to Asher's 6ft 1 presence fitting into my long passageway. He is banishing the spirit of whoever the burglar was. His undemanding, unquestioning arms around me, press me into the nape of his neck. I kiss him and he smells good.

'I'm going to be honest with you Asher. No more faking right?.'

'Ok darling', My hand feels clammy as he guides me to my bed. We lay down, side-by-side, facing each other.

'You know my line of business. I told you I catfish multiple people and honeytrap clients'.

'Mmhmm, including me darling'.

I blush at the unspoken truth.

'Well my best one is from a Taiwanese woman living in Shoreditch. She's called I-wen, or Jo, or Jos in English. I saw you liked one of her posts ages ago. Thing is, she's onto me'.

Asher's blue eyes widen either in wonder or consternation. He's silently listening. I heave his muscly leg over my side.

'Not joking. She was at a bookshop in Croydon in the summer, or spring. It was a warm day anyway. Then the Leeds meeting. She was in the audience. I went to the loo, came back and she had vanished. Then a few nights ago, before I got burgled, she was in the building. I heard a commotion in the passageway and went to look through my peephole. She was fucking standing outside my door'.

Asher breathes out with a look of pity. He kisses my forehead.

'Look, I know you're sleeping with her. I just need to know … I just need to know if she knows about me'.

Asher strokes my hair and pushes the locks behind my ear. He holds my cheek and the look in his eyes turns serious.

'Look. I know her. I think I showed you on my phone in the pub in Elephant and Castle. She added me on Facebook. We got chatting and she told me we were both being catfished'.

The palms of my hand are clammy again. 'What!?'

'Anyway we met up and looked at our fake profiles'.

CATFISH HONEYTRAP

'OK'. I'm neither affirming nor denying the accusation implicit in his voice.

'I was freaked out because she said we would meet in a bookshop for a coffee. Didn't know about bookshops having cafes inside'.

Was it *that* bookshop, when I saw Jos exiting in a hurry? His casual tone is so disarming. With his rough background he must be taking me for some nerdy cat-woman, setting up random profiles to fill the sad whole in my emotional life. I haven't got the heart to tell him my earnings are well into six figures.

'It's ok babe. I still like you. Lots. And there's nothing serious going on between me and Jos'.

So it is Jos. She's westernised after all. I'm saving myself the mental quibbles about how to pronounce 'I-wen'. Future voicenotes for horny men with Asian fetishes can rest on 'Jos', not Ee-when/Eye-when.

'She came over a few nights ago. It's messed up. She's engaged to a long-term boyfriend in Taiwan. She's not staying in England much longer'.

My head is swimming with this information delivered in the comfort of my bed by a man whose word and instincts I have grown to trust. So my catfish is ironically as guilty of the cheating that my alter ego has been honeytrapping for months. She's been getting her bit of western romance before settling down. I bite my lip realising that she must have thought Asher was taking her to Leeds Castle, not a castle near Leeds. As I stare into Asher's eyes, there's no sign of cockiness or triumph. His eyes are wide soulful pits. Maybe Jos has been doing criminal rehabilitation and they would have met each other anyway.

I'm pretty sure she's doing some social work Masters degree. It doesn't feel right to pry any more. I don't want to burst a spell and forego future options on someone who might remain my most successful catfish. Better play it safe and change the subject. I could ask him about his manslaughter charges. But I'll be bolder and ask him about his feelings.

'Have I hurt you Asher?'

'Nah, darling. I got hurt young. You're all freaking mental'.

'Ha fuck off'. Firing back with a profanity is doong the job of deflecting any more inquiries into my confession about catfishing. I'm mental as mental women are mental in general. I'm a token representative of gynolunacy. 'You got hurt young?'

'Mate of mine had a mom. I was only sixteen'.

'You were with an older woman?'

'She was after me for ages. I went to hers because I couldn't get home when it was all snowed in and there were no buses home. She was crying on the bed because she wanted to have sex with me, but didn't want to make me'.

'She what? How old was she?'

'38 or something. She kept going on about not wanting to make me do it for like half an hour. I didn't want to say no to hurt her feelings so I had to but I wish I did say no now because at that point I was a virgin'.

My incredulous smile has turned to a lump in my throat again.

'And she knew I couldn't get home because buses and taxis stopped'.

'I'm sorry Asher'.

'Yeah. I told my first girlfriend about it a year later. She was fuming. But we agreed that I was still a virgin because she was one too. We wanted it to be special'.

I hear his calm voice and feel his thumb caress my cheek.

Chapter 12

I must have slept ten hours. I recall Asher leaving in my slumber. I stretch my arms and got to my desk. When I flap open my laptop again, something new appears. A new message request. There's something different about it. It's blank grey. The profile is completely blank. It's not catfish. It's anonymous, created solely to message me.

'Meet me on Thursday. I know you are fake. Reply to show you understand'.

I can't reason why I'm getting into a conversation with this blank account.

'I'm not lying. I'm not fake. I'm I-wen.'

It's part confessional, part therapeutic, to vomit out all my suppressed schizophrenia. Besides, what the hell does this character want?

Show me proof, crazy bitch

'Proof, what the hell? I've got no idea who I'm talking to. What gives you the right?'

Take a picture of you now holding up your right thumb.

She's onto me. Telling me to do painting by numbers. It should be funny, like a mundane phone sex when some sad sack asks me to put my hand between my legs and I pretend to do it. I blub excuses. I'm busy with breakfast and she's interrupting. I even pull out one of the hongsheng niurou pics I'd stored from a restaurant visit last week when I was impersonating a cook. The Seen icon appears at the side of the immaculate dish. The writing continues. It takes ages, as if she's typing out a court summons. I can't take it. I flap down the laptop. I put the world aside. I abandon the new Twitter account. I stop browsing Tumblr and Facebook altogether. I don't answer the phone. Any texts received are innocent of the fake worlds I've created.

I walk to the kitchen to make coffee. I am nervous. Even though there is nobody else in the house, I shut the door behind me. It's been ages since I've travelled beyond my own post code. I've tried to follow up on promises to do physical PI work but always chicken out. My catfish strike lasts the rest of the day, a bottle of Chardonnay, and all night. I wake in the night with a nightmare fresh in my mind. I'm trying to escape London in a train. All the other passengers turn out to be my catfish targets. Before they can get up to approach me I rush to the end carriage and lock myself in the toilet. The braying, jostling victims crowd outside and rattle away at my bolted door. Then I was crying, gulping and shaking. At 8 am the next morning I push myself up on my elbow, grab my phone from under my pillow and switch off the alarm. The urge grips me again. I have to create new profiles. I have to keep going. Catfishing has become an itch to scratch, like eating, drinking, breathing.

The next morning there's a buzzing sound under Jon's old pillow. I grope my hand under its coolness and flip the phone open. The crazy bitch has called my mobile. How the hell did she get my number? I clamp the phone to my ear, as if it's a landline communication to a spy. The receiver start to moisten with my beads of sweat, whether out of heat or my nervousness I don't know. Then a garbled woman's voice sounds. The tone is silly like a child's toy. I want to penetrate behind the Doppler sound to identify it. But the instruction that comes next makes the moistness on the phone chill. I pause, still trying to absorb how this woman could have known.

It's time to confront her. I forgot to take my washing out last night. As I pull out my near-dry joggers the bobbles under my gripped palms tell me my home clothes have seen better days. The jeans are still damp. As my hand graps the pocket side I panic. I left Jon's letters in there. I pull out the shredded, clumped bits of paper. The smudged ink is the heartless victim of my washing machine and my negligence. Vague memories of Jon's words come to my mind. Some were poems he liked to write, others were love-notes, ideas for a holiday. As I sink to the floor my frustration boils. I'm proud that I no longer care about

CATFISH HONEYTRAP

Jon's keepsakes. But I feel disarmed about the impending meeting with bitchface, if it really is her. I have nothing to prompt myself. I didn't even get round to photographing or photocopying them. I get to my feet, paint my lips red with a steady hand, and take two deep breaths before walking out onto a landing bathed in a powdery pink wintry sunlight.

    I head into town. As I leave my flat I feel as though I have astronaut boots on my feet. Exiting the building I'm thankful for the straight line of pavement leading to the bus stop, and for the momentary absence of people and their stale air pressing against me. As I turn to the bus stop there's the usual homeless man sitting on the knoll of grass opposite. Of all people he looks at me and smiles. Then he puts two fingers in front of his mouth and waggles his tongue grossly. Luckily the bus crawls past and blocks my sight of him. A stench of weed pervades to bus stop, so I wander to the open park area behind. The cool breeze does not clear my head. I wish to be reincarnated as the deadbeat innocent I was nine months ago. I just missed the bus. I huddle down on the bench next to the parkwall. The personalised love carvings are so deep that I can almost feel them imprinting my back. I turn to look at the random hearts and z-ended names, like relics from a pre-internet era. I wonder if I could have launched my business in the old days of dial-up or pre-internet. I would have been offering cryptic notes offering 'relationship healing' pasted at bus stops, phonebooths and pub toilets. A gaggle of pre-teen girls with crinkly hair appear out of nowhere. I get up from the bench and walk to the wall. I place my hands on the ledge at waist height and press myself into one of the alcoves flanked by a shallow iron railing. I feel the cool stone pressed against my gingers and step on to the bottom rung of the railing. I look out to the non-descript street of Costcutters, a busker, and a group of people seeming to be rehearsing a flash-mob. My mouth feels dry as I exhale and face upwards, as if wanting a sign from the white overcast sky. I jolt my head down and allow the brief bloodrush to push me gently over the side of the railing. Part of me wants to hurl myself down. The fall would be enough to fuck me up, if not kill me.

Hey hun, long time no speak. Are you free to meet up for lunch now? Fiona x

What the hell? She ghosts me for weeks and now she summons me, expecting me to drop everything. Part of me wants to avoid my blackmailer and listen to Fiona rattle on about Aaron and her supposedly amazing life. But I don't want to accept or to ignore her: 'Hi Fiona, sorry I'm busy this afternoon. Faye x'.

The blackmailer has texted.

Meet me at the XYZ.

How the hell could she have known about this place? I control my breathing, sitting on the side of the bed. I could really do with a friend right now. Fiona would not judge me.

XYZ is good, I text back.

I want to call whoever it is. But I need to keep my cover. *Send me a pic of you now*, I type. The message stays on 'Seen' for more than ten seconds.

That's a sign I'm being catsfished.

A pic, why?

Amateur. *A pic of you now, just whatever you're doing.* There's a minutelong pause on 'Seen'. Then a photo of some thighs in leggings appear. I post it next to the Facebook photos. I don't know how to superimpose pics but I can see that they don't align.

I feel calmed by the knowledge that my blackmailer, whoever she is, is crap enough to stoop to the sort of depths that have been my playground for the past eight months. She's obviously new to Facebook faking and like anyone who's made a discovery, she must think it's new and clever. She'll notice in time that like me she is a liar and a cheat.

She will cause upset and harm, and attract all the shitposts I get.

CATFISH HONEYTRAP

When I get to XYZ I try to manage my anxiety. Arriving early, but not too early, helps. The sky is uncommonly bright for winter. The faintest warmth from the sun bathes my face, as a group of scarf-wearing Asian tourists hang around the hedge flanking the park holding selfie sticks aloft.

I keep looking down at my phone, scrolling through random text messages, pretending to write some of my own. Then I recall that I had ordered a coffee. I cling to the bar whilst the machines grinds away. My grip on the shelf steadies my mind and my breathing. It's only when I sit down that my world gets all fucked up. Fiona is here, smoking, with the Thames shimmering away behind her. She was supposed to have given up ages ago. Now she's lined up on with fellow smoker exiles on the terrace. There's only glass separating her. But should I hide from her? I really don't want to face my blackmailer when she's here. I don't need her *told you so's* after weeks of ignoring her warnings.

I stride by behind the pillars and the dividing glass draped in plastic foliage. I take a seat with my back to her part of the restaurant, belt and braces in case she happens to see me upon leaving. As I pull up the menu a woman looms around me. Fiona is looking down on me, cupping her elbow in her hand, flicking ash from her cigarette onto the pavement, as if provoking the owners into banning smoking outside, too. She shakes her head and flashes me a self-satisfied, lopsided smile.

I give her a coy wave as she comes inside.

'You stole from me.'

Her calm monotone makes me shiver. She's standing opposite me, bringing the outside cold into her posture. She is gripping the top of the wicker chair so tightly that her fingers go white, accentuating her pink nail varnish.

'What the fuck?'. She can't mean her phone from ages ago when I fled Jake's wandering hands. What else can she mean? Is she sore about how much I'm making now? Does she remember what it's like to be broke?

'You stole my whole story, and my fiancé. Aaron's dumped me'.

I feel blood flow down from my brain. The sudden din of the restaurant crowds my hearing like an oncoming train. I have no words. I feel as if I'm the wrong person receiving her ire, with the wrong brain in my head. I hate her now. She's holding back and she slyly summoned me away from home even though I told her about my anxiety.

'He thought I was the catfish. You didn't even fucking change the details! All the details I told you, the stuff only he and I could have known. And you kept saying it to the other accounts. It's sick. What a complete idiot I was to trust you! And you made money out of me'.

My mind hazes as she pleads her case. I'm not used to seeing Fiona as a victim. She is as indignant as ever.

'Fiona! What the hell? I told you about this every step of the way. You even fucking put the idea in my head and helped me out with it'.

Her imperious stare hardens, like someone being dredged into memories she would rather leave behind. She must have texted me to check I had accepted her meeting.

'The date I set you up with Jake', she says, exhaling with a told-you-so stare.

'Jake?', I reply helplessly. His name was relevant to her, but what does it mean? Could he not take my snub? Did Fiona tell him what I do and maybe he pretended to be me to seduce Aaron? No, none of it makes sense.

'Marco Prendergast', Fiona says with a pointed glance half-way to recovering her to her old condescending self. 'That was him all along'.

'Wait, w-what?'

Her eyeroll returns. 'That night after the pub when you stormed out. You took my phone and must have scrolled in my Linkedin. Marco was one of Aaron's contacts. But it's him. He's been using that profile to chat to women on the sly. Aaron's been catfishing like you'.

CATFISH HONEYTRAP

'Wait, so Aaron, been cheating? Honestly Fiona, I had no idea. It was only words anyway. I never saw this Marco Prendergast up close, never saw his face. Honestly I had no idea it was Aaron.'

'I can't believe you would betray my trust! He found out about it and is convinced I was catfishing him. And those details. Only I could have known them. Now he's dumped me. You've screwed over my life!'

My heart is beating faster and I'm a few seconds behind digesting what she's saying. Right now I want to surrender, not to pretend. I want to stop thinking. It would be great if she could just hit me. My anxiety peaks as I imagine her emptying the glass over my head, or dragging me to the toilet, close enough for her to take me there with ease without anyone noticing.

'He's been cheating on you, Fiona, I had no idea!' My innocence is cutting no ice with her look. She's got dumped by a dick and she's blaming little old me. She's fallen down into my world. I've been here a year already. It's time to go on the attack. She's drying her cheeks with a serviette. I can't think whether they are tears of anger at my betrayal or Aaron's infidelity. I want to think Aaron's to blame. But Aaron Carlton, a man responsible for 80 percent of the tears of the women he encounters, can't be to blame. Fiona stops the tears and refocuses her accusing stare. It's time to go on the offensive.

'What do you mean, other accounts? Why do you think I was saying that to other accounts?'

She eyerolls me. I really want to fucking slap her. It always pisses me off when she does that but the rage would be cathartic. I could storm off and complicate our fight into something more than me creeping out her fiancé. It would be me betraying her weird private life *and then me slapping her*. Right now being known as a violent maniac sits better than trying to confront the layers of lies and half-truths.

'Fiona, you said other accounts.'

'We're linked on Ipads, remember?'. Her stiff-backed stare peered down at me with a sudden facial tilt, as if she's suddenly fifteen and I'm suddenly an evil stepmum.

'Fiona, what the fuck! You've been catfishing me, all this time. That's bullshit about the Ipads. You need to log in'. The words are shredding on my tongue. They shatter as they come out, as if I can't comprehend them myself.

'Don't fucking make this about you! Just because you've been such a narcissist doesn't mean others can't play your game. And to think, I used to pity you'. She punctuates these last words with her pointy forefinger, stabbing the air with each syllable.

All those shitposts about me, the fat-shaming and snarky comments about pizza and alcoholism, all the weeks of abuse. It was Fiona, the whole time. The stupid chav-bun Leonie woman was her. I stand up.

She flinches, as if expecting me to punch her. I have no intention of crying and yet I feel my eyes leaking constantly like rusty taps.

'You think I'm just some overweight loser. You never took me seriously. Whenever we hang out you're always looking over my shoulder for someone slimmer to talk to. And you have no fucking idea what I've made of myself'. I'm aspirating my protests of innocence, as if plucking sentences from the air.

The old saying *seeing red* has never meant anything to me before. But now I understand. I storm off. The rage is making me tremble. I know it's anger coursing through my veins because when I push open the door it swings so fast it almost catches me back in my face. The cold hits me like an upended bucket of water. I will the door to slam a second time behind me. There's a voiceless shame vibrating in my head stopping me from thinking. My teeth chatter violently as I head to the underground. A cold downpour starts plastering my hair to my face. I get on the tube and miss my change. I stay on the Circle Line the long

CATFISH HONEYTRAP

way round, wanting to keep going round in circles all day. Eventually I take the grimy tunnel exit onto my street. When I get off it's already dusk. Maybe this is what ghosts do, returning to the scene of their lives and lies. It's cold but I refuse to put on the coat I'm holding wrapped up in my arm. It's as if I don't deserve to be warm, or as if the cold can dumb the shock of my mutual betrayal. I start the half-mile walk in the direction of my estate, and I flinch as soon as a car revs its engines behind me. The Moon's large face is keeping watch. My temple throbs and my feet feel heavy as I keep walking. My route is programmed into me. Me head continues to throb and my legs feel weak. I perch on a bench by a phone booth and centre myself amidst the rush of traffic and headlights. Then I'm running, running across the road. A passer-by makes a detour around me, and otherwise does not glance in my direction. I don't want to process anything now. I take a deep breath and get to my feet. Muscle memory takes me home.

Chapter 13

Asher's car is on the drive. I feel tense and tiptoe my way upstairs. When I unlock my door I make a beeline for the toilet. I get to my knees and hug the bowl patiently. I feel woozy but there's nothing to heave up. My entire body is laced in a thin layer of sweat. I get up and take a quick shower. I look in my mirror and sob with fury. I smash my fist against the tiled wall untiil my knuckles ache. If I only I could erase the past nine months. Block everyone and everything. Pretend I had never created four dozen profiles. Get a shit job, be another medicore cog in a machine, sleepwalk through life, find a guy, get a Barratt home out of London somewhere. Or stay unemployed and get driven out to some shithole in Kent.

I open my laptops and do routine housekeeping. I want to let my autopilot blot out my thoughts about Fiona and my queasy stomach.

Sandra needs updates. Her messages are blown up by a line of exclamation marks and an angry post on her feed: *Good thing those weren't my pics haha. Stop being a predator and go get a life. No one falls for these tricks!!* I plonk my elbows on my desk and press both eyes into my palms. I google erase rewind identity, but all that comes up is the Cardigans song. I add 'catfish' and see a a link to a forthcoming MTV show, then some links on 'How to spot a catfish'. I flap it down and grab a ginger nut, my best remedy after I've dry-heaved. I open my own Facebook and find only one message. It appears from Asher, the ground zero of my masculine blackmailing.

'you know u can come clean nobodys perfect.'

It takes me a few seconds to take in this non-sentence sentence, without upper cases or punctuation, reeking of authenticity. I'm so used to receiving fuck-yous and other hatemails, sometimes in dissertation length. This one is disarmingly honest. For a few moments I feel weightless, floating like an out-of-body experience. Suddenly I'm

CATFISH HONEYTRAP

a wayward daughter, a renegade come clean, with my entire fake lives ready to burst into flames if I only accept his offer of a light.

Next day Asher has sent me some long texts. I scan it and need to take a moment before I can digest their emotional intensity. A last look at Jos first. Mike has messaged me with two attached photos. They're both from the the original I-wen's Facebook page.

Do you go as I-wen Tai aswell as Chang or am I just tripping
nah this is crazy knew there was something odd about this
This person is not contactable on Messenger.

I exhale and press my cheek into my open palm. Then there's an email from Brian at the FPIUK. *Sorry Faye. I'm afraid the board met after the Leeds conference and the panel decided there are irregularities in your investigative work. We won't be recommending you as a candidate for accreditation at this time. Feel free to reply or arrange a call if you want to learn more details of why we made our decision.* I feel a total loser. I need a hug now. But Asher's messages are all I've got.

'This message is hard to right. I've had a drink and I'm not supposed to. In fact I don't drink at all now since I was inside. You think I'm thick because I was inside. But you're wrong. Two things you need to now about me. I got a proper education inside, with grammar and everything. Second, and this is hard for you to believe. The man I killed was in a fight. I killed him in self-defence. And you wont believe this. But the relatives thanked me after I was sent down. He was a cunt and not missed by anybody'.

'I was going to delete this message because I'm pissed. If I sound like a twat then forgive me. If you don't get it this is fine. Just a diary for me'.

I keep scrolling. I can't remember the last time a man poured his heart out to me.

'Since you messaged me weeks ago with your catfish bollocks my life changed. I never felt this way before about anyone. Noone made me feel like this. I should be pissed you were a catfish all this time. But you're fucked up a bit and it's sweet. I don't care about the money and the scraps you threw me from your table. I think what you're doing is fucked but it works for you. I can be your partner. More than that. I'm into you. I missed our chats and our fucks. I want a relationship with you for real'.

I go upstairs. Taiwanese girl left hours ago. I barge through as he opens the door. None of this is his fault. He never expected me to be the person I've been. Now I can feel normal. My embrace of him breaks all disguise. The firmer I hug his muscular body, the more the recent past disappears. The next few hours of my life will erase the chaos of my memories. I kiss him fully. He pushes me back to his against his door. His tongue runs along the seam of my lips I feel boneless, as if no door and no grip around my waist would have me melt into a puddle. I buck my hips against his body enticing his hand between my legs. He starts rubbing. I moan in response and feel myself moistening. The next hour of my life will be devoted to the unlying senses. All touch, taste and smell. No words or lies can set me back.

*****

As I lay next to him the dusk erodes my view of the bra the Taiwanese girl left hanging on his wardrobe knob. I hear the buzz of my alarm clock go off downstairs. I'm not going to work a catfish shift, but the sudden realisation of my predicament hit me. As I get up I feel my hollowness return to my gut. Asher sleeps so deeply and quietly. I pick up my clothes from the floor. I land my legs through my leggings onto the floor and curl the blouse around me. I glance back at his undisturbed handsome face. Downstairs my shower betrays my calm by blurting out water either too hot or too cold. I spread a showergel lather over my body and do a quick rinse, holding my hair high and dry.

Next day he shows me the evidence I've been suspecting since the big reveal at the XYZ. Fiona hooked him up with the Taiwanese girl months ago.

CATFISH HONEYTRAP

'hey Eminem. I was liking your posts way back. We've got a mutual friend in I-wen'.

'Weird question but have you been chatting to someone pretending to be her?'

What do you mean?

'Just that I-wen added me after I was liking her posts. Then I found somewhere was catfishing her. The catfish added you'.

!?

'This is her her anyway. She's a faker.'

I read the thread without breathing, scanning down to see if any of her words mention me by my real name. I click on the link. The fake I-wen profile I have built up over the past eight months explodes into view on a foreign device as is she were a piece of forensic evidence. Mortification creeps up my spine as I see my handiwork as if I were a third person.

Hey sorry. I don't know you or this woman.

'I know it's weird but could you message her? I mean the real I-wen'.

That is a weird ask

'Sorry hun, but it just bothered me when I saw the faker. I've got a boyfriend who's been doing something similar'.

It's a very weird ask

'I messaged I-wen. She knows she's been catfished. She'll really appreciate it if you reach out and tell her your contact isn't her'.

So that was it. My catfishing led to their real relationship and my best friend was working behind my back for months.

I'm going to pull the plug. I need to drive my new sense of moral indignation to a conclusion. I go down to my flat and feel a dormant bung of tears and snot well up in my face. TV drama images flash in my mind of me making a police confession. *I think I have accidentally initiated an extortion racket of entrapping people across London and the Home Counties and making over £100,000 investigating affairs that never existed.* Maybe the police would find the time to come over and detain me for questioning. Or maybe my scam is worth only a caution from a Community Support Officer, or a blacklisting from Brian at the FPIUK. It would have been a hilarious story to tell Fiona, if I hadn't destroyed her life in the process.

As I sit at my desk a sinking feeling seizes me that there are dozens of Fionas whose lives I've turned upside down. The three faceless computer screens stare at me accusingly. I word a group message for all my targets. My laptop is configuring something and there's a delay between my typing and the words appearing. My hands are shaking and it takes me a while to notice that I've typed wrong. Then I delete wrong, swear, and get roped into a nervous cycle of typing and retyping. I take a deep breath and finish the apology. I copy and paste it to the sent contacts from frumpy I-wen down to the sockpuppets. I do the same for all the other catfishers and feel righteous calm as I destroy the past nine months of my hard work and livelihood. There are at least four accounts I suspect are Fiona's. I'm glad they will get the same message. It can count as a non-apology apology from me.

I'm sorry to be the bearer of bad news. I'm afraid I have engaged with you under false pretenses. This account is fake. You do not really know me. But I am diagnosed with Obsessive Compulsive Disorder and Agoraphobia. I am seeking help with my issues and I am sorry for any hurt or disgust caused to you. You will not be hearing from me again.

I flap down the laptop, triumphantly exhaling. My strenuous composure was proof of my honesty. And I know I've played a confidence trick. I'm experienced enough with MSN to know that a depersonalised statement longer than three sentences is less likely to be read. I knock both other laptops to the floor and let rip a joyous sigh. I am elated by a sense of nothingness. I have been rejected and have rejected in turn. I am in glorious freefall. I go straight to bed and sleep the sleep of the saved.

The next morning I wake to see I have slept for 11 hours. My Parsnip phone has been buzzing with with redirected calls to my NHS

CATFISH HONEYTRAP

Direct kind of automated reply: *Thank you for calling. I'm sorry that we are currently receiving a high volume of calls.* I check all accounts, scrolling through each to find more than half saw the message, only a few had blocked me, and about the same number replied. There is no pattern in the location of responses. Some north of the river, some in Croydon, one in Brighton, two in Guildford, a few in Kent. Husbands, boyfriends, businessmen, women, all real people with lives and troubles, whose vulnerability, greed and curiosities I have abused for months. Now it is my turn to be upfront and vulnerable.

The few who have bothered to respond are more mixed than I was expecting. One says *give me back my money, bitch!* before blocking me in an indignant own goal. One replies LOL and another with a giggle emoji followed by a block. Some are clichéd, saying *you need help* and *I have no words.* My throat feels heavy when I see a terse reply from Joe Schmitt: *You have no shame.* The poor man had developed an online relationship with a real woman who still never properly existed.

Another invites me to go fuck myself. If only he had the decency to remember that that's what I did with him last month when he thought I was bitchface and I kept the webcam facing the lower half of my body. Quite a few coming from the most wankerish targets were funny. They seemed to have read only the first or last sentence, as if I was giving a suicidal cry for help: *Let me know if I can help* and *It sucks. Don't know what to say.*

I breathe out in relief and make coffee. The harm is done and confessed. I let the travesty linger until I have my filter coffee in hand. One or two new replies do not change the overnight pattern. Without any ceremony, I block each target before deleting each account. The truth is penetrating my mind, for the first time in months. I am spared a public *mea culpa*. I'm thirty next month and I'm not going to overthink the last year of my twenties. There comes a point where too much has happened, too much water under the bridge. And it was all online, mostly. There's no baying crowd outside waiting to yell and spit at me.

There's only one more demon to exorcise. I create a throwaway gmail account: faye740, based on Google's elimination of the previous 739 women with my name. I wonder how many other random Fayes are floating in the online world, and whether any of them are about to confess to an ex-boyfriend who broke their heart.

It was me all along. You hurt me but I'm sorry for all the stalking. I'm OK now and I have stopped for good. Have a great life Parsnip Jon. Faye x

Fiona's blocked me and Asher's is the only face I have to see when I tell him the truth of everything that happened. Only now do I notice how anxious I have been, constantly worried, always braced for some devastating investigation. Almost animal-like dread stalked me whenever I left my flat. But now I feel relief. The online world loses its hold over me. I am blood, flesh, nerves and tendons, whole once again. I sit on the couch next to Asher. He's leaning back with his feet propped on the coffee table. I naturally lean into him, like we're a couple. He pulls me against his chest and we just sit there in silence. His coarse thumb is brushing the nape of my neck. I know this is his silent way of telling me he is here for me.

I wake up with Asher's arm around me. I'm not sure why he's on the phone at 6 in the morning. It's a woman's voice. The Taiwanese woman is dumping him from 8 hours ahead. I log on to the fake gmail I set up yesterday. Jon's replied. *If this is a joke. It's not a funny one. Go away.* I do not budge as Asher ends his call. I re-read the terse email over and over. Is he claiming that what happened didn't really happen? Or does he acknowledge my stalking and want to send me to Coventry?

'The I-phone I had got nicked. Picked up this old brick instead darling'.

Asher flashes me an old Nokia and lays on his side next to me.

'Can't be arsed with a newer model. I don't miss the instant communications any more. Got you now darling. I'm liking the slower pace of life'.

CATFISH HONEYTRAP

A tear moistens my eye. I want to rewind fifteen years, before Wifi, before internet. Before the virtual world had crept into my every thought. Down-to-erath Asher with his basic brickphone is my escape to nostalgia.

'You ok darling?'.

'I'm fine. I don't know why I'm crying'.

'Have you blocked your profiles?'

'Can we talk about something else please?'. That window of clarity, of coming clean, has passed. I want the curtains of privacy to cloak me. I roll onto my side and feel his body envelop me. His breath breezes across my cheek as a heavy bus trundles past faintly rattling his window. I squeeze my eyes shut, just as his rough fingers brush my skin, up to my shoulders.

After three days the calm envelops me. It's occurring to me now that the burden of living four dozen fake lives and cutting them loose are entirely different mental states. I feel lighter walking down the street. My online creations have taken their final bow. They've exited the stage like the actors they were, now receding into figments of my imagination. The sensation of having missed my real life all these months is creeping up on me. I can make good money again, doing something honest. But I have time to think. I start exercising on my yoga mat. Asher cooks me meals and we bedhop before I wake from eight hours of sleep. We fold the blanket together, enclosing our lovestained sheets for washing, a manoeuvre that makes me feel like a couple in the making. The night sky darkening our window resets my life.

I accept an add from a Fiona-less contact from years back, a girl called Emily with whom I used to proofread university coursework. She takes precisely zero shits. This is my future and my present. The parallel lives of the past months are no longer mine. Cynicism and shame, my faithful companions over the past year, have fucked off. After months of screen-blinded reclusion a lightness returns to my shoulders. I have six figures and a six-foot boyfriend with a six pack. I am secure.

Don't miss out!

Visit the website below and you can sign up to receive emails whenever Camren Walker publishes a new book. There's no charge and no obligation.

https://books2read.com/r/B-A-EUKBD-LQTLF

BOOKS 2 READ

Connecting independent readers to independent writers.

About the Author

Camren Walker is a married writer, parent and dog-owner living near London, UK. Watch out for the next titles in the *Confessional Thriller* series!